WASH ASHORE

ASH⊙RE

a tale of Cape Cod

Mary Petiet

To Jerry

Enjoy Cape Cod

xo MP

Mary Petrit

Also by Mary Petiet

WASH ASHORE

a tale of Cape Cod

MARY PETIET

Sea Crow Press
amplifying voices

Sea Crow Press
Wash Ashore: A Tale of Cape Cod
Copyright © 2022 by Mary Petiet

Wash Ashore is a work of fiction. Names, characters, businesses, places,
events, locales, and incidents are either the products of the author's
imagination or used in a fictitious manner. Any resemblance to actual
persons, living or dead, or actual events is purely coincidental. However, the
issue of land preservation is very real on Cape Cod.

Trade Paperback ISBN: 978-1-7358140-7-0
Ebook ISBN: 978-1-7358140-8-7
Library of Congress Control Number: 2022933097

Cover Image by Alasdair Petiet
Cover Design by Popkitty Design
Interior Formatting by Mary Petiet

www.seacrowpress.com

For those who work to preserve Cape Cod

Chapter One

EACH DEATH, small or big, can be said to mark the end of a particular universe. At 10:30 on a busy April morning in the center of Cape Cod's North Bay Village, the universe ended for Eartha Fullerton as she fell dead of a heart attack in the post office. She must have been as surprised as everyone else that early spring day as she crumbled, dropped her mail, and left the premises in the most definite way possible. There was nothing anyone could do, and it was over before the ambulance arrived from the fire station across the street. The hospital recorded her dead on arrival, aged 85, and the postmaster made sure the entire village knew about it well before lunch that afternoon.

Two days later, ancient Peter Souza peered across the street at Eartha's house, Silver Beech. He was one of Eartha's few surviving contemporaries, and had been gamely setting out to plant a packet of seeds he was sure would win the fall pumpkin contest as the first cars pulled up. He'd expected the family to arrive and thought to go over with sympathy as soon as the seeds were in and to turn over the care of Eartha's insistently hungry cat to its relations. He would miss Eartha, but in the pragmatic way of the very old, he assumed good-naturedly he'd probably be joining her soon anyway.

THE AIR WAS alive with salt as Olive Adams parked under the Silver Beech tree, unfolded herself from the car, and slowly closed the door beneath the great branches. The tree had always welcomed her upon arrival at her aunt Eartha's sprawling house, and this time was no different—except for the absence of Eartha. Otherwise, all was the same. The gardens and porch lay unchanged, and the summers spent here with Eartha hummed through her head as her mother, gray-haired and immaculately dressed, ran out to hug her.

"Honey, you're just in time!" Rose said.

Her mother took in her red hair pulled back in a simple ponytail and her teary green eyes and held her tight. Olive looked warm in her favorite comfy sweater, an old Aran she'd worn nearly into submission, and her jeans and boots gave her a casual air. Eartha's big black cat, Rasputin, wove his way between the two as they hugged, and mewed plaintively behind them as they climbed the porch steps and walked around back to the kitchen.

The house was in business mode as they joined Olive's dad Stephen at the big table with an official-looking man and a large pile of paperwork. He introduced his companion as local lawyer Johnson Henly, Esq., and handed Olive a cup of coffee. Rasputin concluded the introductions with a light-ning streak through the cracked door, across the table, and straight for the stacked papers. Things were happening quickly: reading the will and planning the funeral, and the drive down from Boston hadn't been nearly enough time to think through the two days since Olive had received news of Eartha's death.

John Henly, Esq., fended off the cat and recovered without missing a beat.

"As you know, you three are the only remaining family," he said.

Rasputin retreated to a high shelf to observe proceedings as he tried to identify the interlopers in his kitchen. Olive surveyed the room. It hadn't been updated since about 1935. It was so old you could make a fair case it had returned to style: the ancient wood-burning stove holding court across the table from the 1950s gas range, the free-standing cupboards and tables predated fixed counters, and the soapstone sink under the east-facing window glowed each morning with the sunrise. Her reverie was cut short as the cat lost patience, leaped from the shelf to the table with a definitive mew, and the papers flew in all directions as Johnson Henley, Esq.'s coffee spilled just shy of his lap.

Olive nearly missed what he said next in a strangled voice. "As her youngest surviving relative, Eartha left Silver Beech to you, Olive."

THE FOLLOWING SATURDAY, they sent Eartha off from a crowded church, with flowers from the local garden club and refreshments by the North Bay Historical Society.

The spring sun filled the elegantly plain New England church. High ceilings reached to the sky, and rows of tall windows welcomed the light. The air in the church was sweet with flowers, creating a greenhouse effect perfect for Eartha, who had always been happiest with her hands in the soil. It was a rare sunny day for the time of year: on Cape

Cod, spring is elusive, a mostly non-existent season, fog-shrouded and rainy until it seems someone turns on the heat, and summer arrives overnight. The minister led a service of memories celebrating Eartha, and the choir sang *Morning Has Broken*. As everyone joined in, the church was filled with music for those few minutes, and the singers were filled with togetherness, even if they'd have been hard-pressed to define it.

In the crowded church hall afterward, Olive's mother was touched by the number of guests. And because funerals are for the living as well as the dead, she was finding the whole event an unexpected trip down memory lane.

"Rose, I heard it was completely unexpected," a voice murmured in her ear, as a hand landed gently on her arm.

"Betsy Graham!" The two old school friends hugged tightly.

"Why does it take a thing like this for people to see each other?" Besty said.

Soon a group had gathered, friends from school days and long-ago summers.

"Remember the time Eartha saved the skunk with the tin can stuck on its snout at the cocktail party? I was helping out that night and damned if she didn't walk right up, ease that can off, and let the skunk go right back into the woods," said Wren Haskell.

"That's right! Legend of the summer! I was there too, and I've never seen a party go so quiet so fast. You could hear the skunk slip into the bushes. What if it had sprayed?" said Betsy.

They laughed. They had reached that point where the tension gives a bit and the memories can flood in and the old stories can feel good. Rose and her friends were all a good 15 years younger than Eartha. Rose had been a late arrival to the family and had looked up to her big sister.

"But do you remember, she rode a motorcycle to the party because her car wouldn't start?" Rose said.

They laughed again. There was no dearth of good Eartha stories—she had lived a full life.

"Remember her old horseshoe crab costume for the Fourth of July parade?" Davey Smith said.

"Won third prize the year she covered it with flowers," Olive's dad Stephen joined the conversation.

"Remember the time she was 'rescued at sea' by the environmental police? Her engine had frozen coming onto the flats and they had seen her land the boat, and wouldn't let her just get any old tow," said Dell Sears.

"That's right! Made her tie her boat behind and sit right up in the bow of their launch in one of those bright orange life jackets!" said Vick Easton.

"And she was spitting nails by the time they got into the harbor!" Rose said.

The universe that had been Eartha would live on in their memories, which must be what sparked the speculation: would Olive take on the house that had been so much a part of their departed friend?

"We can ask her ourselves," Rose said as Olive came towards them with a coffee pot.

"Honey, what are your thoughts about Silver Beech?"

It was a deer in the headlights moment. Olive hadn't thought. There had been too much to do and too many people to see. But as Eartha's friend Pete Souza caught her eye and smiled, she was reminded how unique a place North Bay was.

Chapter Two

By HERSELF IN Eartha's house after the funeral, Olive was surprised to find she wasn't alone there. Someone else, some*thing* else was there, too, though not in a frightening way. Something was calling her attention just out of view from the corner of her eye, a soft insistence, an invitation, a quiet taking by the hand and leading to—something.

Later, back in the city, she wondered if she could live on Cape at Silver Beech year-round. It was no small thing to think about leaving Boston. She was a city creature, and when she thought about the Cape, it was about visiting Eartha, and when she thought again, it was about childhood summers, warm sand flats, full moon nights, and exuberant gardens. She had always been content among the brick streets of Beacon Hill and fond of her downtown office, where she directed the monthly publication *Boston Today Magazine*. There was not a happening or event in Boston outside of her purview, and she enjoyed getting the story behind each of them as much as she enjoyed the socializing it required.

But something was calling her to the Cape, and while she was watering the plants in her fourth-floor walk-up apartment in the city, she imagined the gardens at Silver Beech, which must have been mature even when Eartha was young. She could see herself growing bumper crops of tomatoes and hear the wind through the trees. She thought about how she had helped organize Eartha's funeral in a daze, but as the fog lifted and she had remained on in the house for a bit after her parents left, she had become comfortable. She began to think she could stay. It hadn't felt like an empty house, and there were worse places to wash ashore, after all.

"OLIVE, YOU LOOK MARVELOUS!" Johnny Gilmore said.

Known as the darling of Beacon Hill, her Boston neighbor was one of the city's most sought-after interior designers. Johnny was an expert in decorative restoration, and a living room by Johnny Gilmore was a living room that had arrived.

Now he held her at arm's length and looked carefully into her eyes. His blonde hair was pushed back in a wave and cropped at the sides, his Ralph Lauren jacket fit his spare frame perfectly, and his loafers were worn down in just the right way. His blue eyes looked concerned, and Olive was reminded why the matrons of Beacon Hill couldn't get enough of him.

"I'm alright, Johnny," she said.

She ordered a white wine spritzer and Johnny asked for a Heineken. The bar on Boston's Chestnut Street was bustling with the Friday after-work crowd and they were lucky to get a seat. Johnny was in his element in the cheerful confusion, and Olive welcomed the distraction.

"Just think about the antiques! I've got a lady on Pinkney Street looking for a Peter Hunt cupboard for her dining room. It's an urban-rustic retreat kind of vibe, a bit of toile, a lot of flowers, big French doors. What's in your aunt's house, anyway?"

"I don't think any Peter Hunt, you might have to go to the source for that, see if there's anything left in P-town."

Peter Hunt was a folk artist who had painted furniture in the northern French peasant style in Provincetown on the Cape around 1950. A lucky designer could sometimes score an old piece, but they'd become rare as time went on.

"But what's in the house?" Johnny persisted.

"That's what I'm trying to figure out. It's chock-a-block full of everything, Eartha's things, and my grandparents' things. My mother grew up there, too, and it hasn't really ever changed. It's a time capsule." Olive watched Johnny lick his chops at the idea of such treasure and smiled.

"Are you leaving the Hill?" he asked abruptly.

"Yes, I told the magazine today. They're keeping me on as a contributor, I can do that from the Cape with a laptop."

He took the news with a sip of beer. "Then we must move you down there and make sure it's fine," he said. "This calls for dinner!"

They ordered steak and spent the evening planning a kind of future. Johnny wasn't losing a great neighbor so much as gaining a foothold in the antique haven of Cape Cod. He anticipated summer estate sales and early bird yard sales, scoring pieces for city clients. He also wanted to spend time with Olive, to make sure she was okay down there in what really were the sticks.

"I'm putting the apartment on the market Monday morning. I'd like to be at Silver Beech by the end of June to get the most of the Cape summer," said Olive. It had been years since she'd had a Cape summer. She was looking forward to it.

"It's April 25 now, that's just over eight weeks," said Johnny. The designer in him took over.

"Weed out of as much stuff as you can, and we'll haul the rest down in my van. Last week of May?"

"Can do. But about what's in the house. I'm not sure. There's a presence. You'll have to come see. Or maybe the word is feel. The house isn't empty, but not in a bad way." Johnny had never known Olive to talk like that.

"Let's go down tomorrow," he said.

THEY ROLLED down the windows of the delivery van as they crossed the Sagamore Bridge to Cape Cod and savored the sea air. Johnny's brown van dated to at least 1960 and carried the legend "Johnny Gilmore Interiors." Johnny used it to haul furniture and fabric and all the accoutrements of a business dedicated to dressing up the city's old houses. If they lucked into a yard sale this trip and found treasure, they'd be ready.

The view from the bridge showed the canal, the blue of the bay, and a stretch of scrub forest as they descended to the Mid-Cape Highway.

"Coming down for the summer, this is where the trip always got exciting," Olive said.

Six more exits and they'd be at Silver Beech.

"Let's take 6A in case there are any yard sales," Johnny said, pulling off at Exit one.

"What's your first memory of Silver Beech?"

Olive knew right away.

"Hurricane Bob. Almost blew us away. We were afraid we'd lose the beech tree, and somehow that seemed like it would be the worst possible luck. At one point, the wind went counterclockwise around the house like the cyclone in the *Wizard of Oz*. We lost power for a week, but the tree is still there," she said.

They were heading east through Sandwich, the sun was warm, and there was not a yard sale in sight.

"We must have gone down to weather the storm with Eartha. My parents were there too. My mother grew up there, so I have her stories as well. Her mother remembered the iceman delivering blocks of ice in the summer, and she remembers the milkman coming in a white suit and giving her an ice cream cup. My grandparents bought the house in the thirties, and we've been there ever since. I used to come down from Wellesley, where my dad was teaching, to spend my summers with Eartha. I loved it," Olive said.

Suddenly Johnny slammed on the brakes, just managing to avoid a flock of turkeys in the road. Olive remembered how Eartha had always insisted the turkeys were escapees from a farm in Western Mass. Maybe they were.

"Damn! Tell them to wait for Thanksgiving!" Johnny said.

The trees formed a canopy of tender green leaves over the street as they got closer to the house. The low-roofed antique Cape houses hugged the landscape, and the travelers caught glimpses of the water beyond the trees and fields. Boston seemed far away.

Old Pete Souza had just checked in on Eartha's cat, Rasputin, when Johnny's furniture van pulled into the driveway at Silver Beech. By now, the cat had resigned himself to life between Eartha's house and Pete's, and he was

11

becoming increasingly comfortable across the street at Pete's. Pete didn't mind, as long as the cat didn't get fancy ideas about digging up his pumpkin seeds. So far the seeds had failed to germinate. Maybe it was still too chilly. The Cape's failure to warm up quickly in spring made most gardeners impatient and was known to wreak havoc with plants put out too early.

The first thing Johnny noticed was the silver beech. It owned the front yard. He parked the van in front of the barn around the back, grabbed their overnight bags, and made for the back door. Olive had mentioned Cape Codders never use the front door, and right now the back was unlocked. The tree murmured as they entered the house, and Johnny found himself in decorator paradise.

"I know! And the real charm is that none of it was intentional. This house evolved," Olive responded to Johnny's awestruck silence.

She shrugged. Even she couldn't explain it.

The kitchen floor was flagstone. The cookstove could still hold a fire. The soapstone sink was to die for. Johnny had clients who would give their eye teeth for such details. And he hadn't even left the kitchen.

Olive was in the pantry rooting out some coffee. Sets of vintage china lined the shelves, and a wide sink and counter provided backup space for entertaining.

Johnny imagined the parties.

Olive set the coffee on and told him to go have a look at the place.

Most of the house's life occurred in the kitchen. Two front rooms, a living room, and a dining room flanked a wide front hall with a broad stairway. Both rooms were well appointed, but a bit formal for daily life. "The rugs alone!"

he thought. A library with leather furniture and a fireplace was tucked behind the living room; a feminine touch showed in the flowered curtains.

This was the kind of house that matures over time. It had a look almost impossible to achieve in a deliberate redecoration. He was glad he had brought his sketch pad, and he would have to take some pictures with his phone. He was completely inspired.

THEY HAD coffee at the kitchen table as Olive browsed leisurely through a pile of accumulated mail. She stopped at a manila envelope addressed to Eartha from the Town of North Bay Historic Preservation Society.

Johnny was planning a trip to the village for provisions.

"We need some seafood. Let's get some swordfish and a nice bottle of white for dinner. Where's the fish market? I can't believe you've been keeping this place up your sleeve all this time. Why am I only just seeing this?"

She began to slit the top of the manila envelope with the handle of the sugar spoon.

"Maybe there are some yard sales further down Cape. We could have a beach picnic for lunch. It's warm enough. And if it rains on Sunday, we can poke around the house. There's history here!"

She pulled out a single slip of white paper and was flummoxed to see it was a notice that the Nickerson land, the 15-acre plot next door to Silver Beech, was slated for total clearing by something called Moraine Land Development, LLC, represented by someone called Douglas Dunn. The Preservation Society was meeting in two Wednesdays to determine if the proposed development fell within their rules to preserve the historic characteristics of the village.

"If it gets chilly we can lay a fire in the old cookstove. It still burns, right?"

Olive took a sip of her coffee and handed the notice to Johnny.

She looked out from the porch at the tangled woods of the Nickerson land beyond the garden. She felt cold air move through the kitchen, chilling her bones.

"Did you feel that? The chill? That's what I meant, there's something in the house," she said.

Chapter Three

ANN MARSTON WAS HAVING a rotten day. The *Boston's Best* clam chowder awards had been announced and her restaurant, The Quahog Connection on Boston's waterfront, had failed to achieve notice. Again. This was her eighth attempt. She knew her chowder recipe was becoming an obsession, and she was struggling to put a good face on the situation as the kitchen cranked up for the lunchtime rush.

She had been involved with The Quahog Connection in several capacities since she dropped out of Boston University to go to culinary school ten years ago. Now she owned the restaurant, and those BU days seemed idyllic when she looked back on them from the hot kitchen. Back then she just ate chowder like anyone else, now she wanted to master the recipe.

A busboy came tearing into the kitchen full throttle, slamming into a server bearing a loaded tray. French fries, fish, dishes, silverware, and her prize-defying chowder crashed to the floor in a slippery, jagged mess. No one seemed hurt and everyone was shouting until Ann hollered for quiet, including the radio. An uneasy calm descended, and she stomped off while her kitchen staff cleaned up and started over.

She stood on the upstairs deck overlooking the harbor, a small, forlorn figure in cook's whites and a pair of kitchen crocs. Her dark hair was cut short for convenience and she was strong from restaurant work. She remembered when she had been less stressed and loved being in the kitchen. She lit a cigarette, reflecting vaguely that she really must stop smoking, and ignored her ringing cell phone.

Deep breath. Watch the seagulls. Don't worry about profit ending up on the floor, lack of professional staff, the sous-chef's propensity for drink, and the annual non-winning of the *Boston's Best* chowder award. Another breath. The crazy busy summer season was just a few months away, and she needed a vacation. She needed to leave The Quahog Connection in good hands and spend at least a month somewhere quiet. Her cell phone rang again and this time she answered it.

Olive could hear the seagulls as soon as Ann picked up.

"Where are you?" she asked.

Ann scanned the sky, her eye following the gull's peaceful flight. The ocean never failed to calm. She tossed her cigarette butt.

"On the back deck at The Connection. Taking a breather. I need a breather," she said.

"That's why I called. Come down to the Cape, stay with me in my aunt's old house for a bit. Let the ocean and the quiet work their magic." Olive said.

"How did you know?"

"I knew. I need some backup down here, and you need

some quiet. Let's be roommates again," Olive said. They had been best friends since their first year at Boston University.

"How soon can I come?" Ann asked.

JOHNNY COULDN'T GET ENOUGH of the house and had a hard time leaving on Sunday night. Olive found it hard to go too, and by the time they got into the old delivery van to cross the bridge once more, she was committed to moving. Even her parents were delighted. She'd be closer to them now that they had retired further down Cape in Truro.

Earlier that weekend it had been damp and gray, as the Cape Cod spring intended. The air smelled of salt, and Olive was happy her Aran sweater was pretty much water-proof. Old Pete Souza had come over to talk about the cat, Rasputin, just as Johnny was unearthing an old Ford in the barn.

"That's Loki," Pete said.

"The car?" asked Johnny.

"Yes, the car. Eartha got it for a song sometime in the '60s. It was old then. Named it Loki because it would either start or not start. You could never tell which. When it did start, it sure cut a good figure on the road, though."

Olive was amazed she had never noticed it before, and she wondered what else they were going to turn up.

"Pete, you've been here for years, right?" she said.

"A lifetime."

"What can you tell us about Silver Beech?"

Pete could remember about as far back as 1945. He was born the year the war started and his dad had shipped out with the Merchant Marine. He thought he could remember

VE Day, and he could remember his dad coming home after those long years.

"I grew up with Eartha. I'm 15 years older than your mother," he said.

"A gramophone! Records!" Johnny called from the barn.

"Did you get notice about the Nickerson land?" Olive asked, glancing over at the property as she spoke.

"Yes! That's what I came over to talk about, I remember now. And Rasputin."

A scratchy foxtrot echoed from the barn.

"The Nickerson land was held in trust for years and years, starting before I was born. No one has ever touched that land as far as I know." Pete took his cap off and absent-mindedly scratched the back of his head as he contemplated the snarled undergrowth. "It was part of an off-Cape trust, then last year it went on the market. I guess the trust dissolved? Moraine Development bought it. Never heard of them before, but I knew it meant trouble. The development part. I have heard of Douglas Dunn, though. They call him The Axe on account of his penchant for that new cologne. Also because of how he works to develop everything that's not nailed down. Watched him grow up meaner and meaner, and I know he has a thing against Lars Salo, the guy over in town hall working to preserve the land here."

The foxtrot gave way to Glenn Miller.

"This is great stuff!" Johnny called.

"The marsh and then the water is at the back of the property, just like at Silver Beech. There's 15-acres of wilderness in there, not much like that left anywhere on Cape these days. It's pretty much an intact ecosystem. Always has been."

"The meeting is scheduled for next Wednesday. I need

to sort things out in Boston, and then I'm coming down Friday. I'm going to town hall for some details about what they can and can't do to the land. Will you come to the meeting and speak against development?" Olive said.

"Already planning to," said Pete.

The cat announced himself with a high-pitched mew as the music flushed him out of the normally quiet barn.

"Now about Rasputin," Pete smiled at his prancing antics, "I'll keep him till you get back."

"Thanks, Pete. I'm coming back to stay," Olive said as she crouched down to scratch Rasputin's head.

Vera Lynn started crooning from the barn about the White Cliffs of Dover, but Olive was seeing seagulls instead of bluebirds.

"Sorry we didn't find any yard sales, Johnny," Olive said later. They were heading back to the city, blissfully traffic-free.

"There was plenty to see at the house, not to worry," said Johnny. He was returning to Boston with a full sketchbook of ideas and a phone stashed with pictures.

"I couldn't bring myself to ask Pete if the house was haunted. But I feel something, and it's insistent." Olive said.

They were clearing the Braintree Split as the highway veered toward Boston. Soon they'd see the downtown skyline, and Beacon Hill was just beyond.

"Ok, I felt it too. I don't know what it is, but it's damp and chilly, right?"

"Yes, and it gets chillier when the Nickerson land comes up."

"Olive, I want to catalog the stuff in your house. It's a

gold mine. Do you really know what's there? I could come down on weekends and document everything. Some of it might be valuable or belong in a museum. And I think we need to find the house's story."

"We do?"

"It's just a hunch. But yes, I think we do," said Johnny.

Chapter Four

IT WAS easy enough for Olive to sublet her Beacon Hill apartment. She rented it for six months to a researcher at the Boston Athenaeum who was renovating his own house just outside of town. He took it furnished, so the changeover wasn't nearly as hard as she'd imagined. She began to make her way to the Cape early that Friday morning, armed with a large cup of Dunkin's and fortified with a blueberry muffin from DeLuca's Market. It's never easy to leave a place where you've been happy, but she told herself she could always come back, she had simply sublet the place, and that made it easier.

She arrived mid-morning in the sunshine. It was the second week of May, and spring was finally taking hold. She imagined the ocean around the Cape warming up and lending the land its warmth. The front lawn was a carpet of daffodils and the silver beech was thinking about leafing. She found her mother working in the garden, a sun hat over her hair and a pair of gloves on her hands. Olive smiled, remembering how Eartha would just charge out bareheaded and sink her hands into the soil without a thought.

"Looks good, Mom!" she called.

"Will you look at the daffodils! Hi, Honey, let's have an iced tea on the porch," her mother replied.

They sat in the old wicker chairs overlooking the Nickerson land.

"I think Peter Souza had a thing for your aunt, years ago," Rose said.

Somehow Olive wasn't surprised.

"I don't remember what happened. They were already teenagers when I was born."

The view from the porch took in half the lawn and a good part of the Nickerson land. The air was alive with birdsong, the daffodils nodded in the breeze, and a pack of squirrels jumped across the tree branches. Everything was energized by the spring sunlight.

"Mom, what's in this house?"

Rose shrugged. "Everything. My parents, the Fullertons, lost their business in the Depression. I don't think you've heard this, have you? You wouldn't remember them. They lived in Gloucester, north of Boston. Dad owned a tuna canning factory, but when he lost it, they decided to move to the Cape. If you can believe it, that was the cheaper option back then. So when they came here around 1935, they brought everything from the old Gloucester house. And they continued to accumulate. So everything might not be an exaggeration."

"But Mom, what is in the house? Sometimes I feel something. I don't remember it from my summers here. Have you felt anything?"

"Every house on Cape Cod is haunted, Honey, haven't

you heard?" Rose laughed.

A fair-weather cloud covered the sun for a brief moment. Rose sipped her tea. The daffodils bobbed in the breeze and Rasputin's tail was just visible among them as he crept through the flowers on his way to the woods beyond.

"Have you heard about the Nickerson land?" Olive nodded toward the woods beyond the garden.

"Pete was here first thing telling me about it. I'm coming to the meeting on Wednesday. I may not live here now, but I certainly grew up here and want to keep the land intact."

"That's three of us, then," Olive said.

JOHNNY ARRIVED in the old brown moving van later that day with armloads of tulips, a wealth of beautiful food, and a case of wine. He unloaded it all into the pantry and busied himself arranging flowers for the house. His provisions included several hardcover notebooks and plenty of space on his phone for pictures. He made salmon on toast points for lunch with Olive and Rose and then got to work cataloging. He started in the library, where he was intrigued by the shelves of books—especially the leather-bound ones.

"My dad used to work here. He did real estate back in the day. It's just so much old stuff. But let me know what you find," Rose said.

Johnny had his nose in a geography book so old its maps stopped at the Mississippi River. Rose took a look.

"That's my great-great grandfather's name on the flyleaf," she said.

"Imagine books so old!" Johnny was in his element. He examined and noted each volume one by one. This could take years and yield riches. He might manage half of the first shelf before dinner. He was planning to roast a chicken and serve it at the big kitchen table.

Ann arrived before dinner. She had left The Quahog Connection in the capable hands of her head cook. On the drive down to the Cape, she wondered why she hadn't taken a break a lot sooner. Maybe the time hadn't been right. In the end, it had been so easy to arrange, it must be right, she told herself. She was going to spend a few months on the Cape with Olive. She had brought enough clothes and a bathing suit in case it warmed up and—most important—her working notes for her evolving chowder recipe. She couldn't wait to see the kitchen at Silver Beech.

DINNER WAS candlelit roast chicken among the tulips. Rasputin the cat must have smelled the food; he arrived while they were serving as one summoned.

"That marvelous cat! I suppose he's using up his nine lives crossing the street between here and old Pete's," said Johnny.

"Well his name's Rasputin, he has at *least* nine lives," said Olive.

"I wonder what tales he could tell us," Johnny mused.

"Yes, no kidding! And have you ever wondered what cats stare at?" Olive said.

Even as they spoke, Rasputin was transfixed by something no one else could see between the counter and the ceiling. The chill was there again. Johnny had felt it in the library earlier that day as well. He wasn't particularly alarmed—he knew old houses had their quirks.

"I think it's got to do with the library. It's always cold there. The rest of the house is only cold sometimes," he said.

Rasputin stared and the candles flickered.

"Have you *seen* anything here or just *felt* it? Is this part of the backup you mentioned needing?" Ann thought for a moment. "Remember my parents' house in Marblehead?"

Olive laughed, there had been some pretty good parties at Ann's house in Marblehead when they were both freshmen at Boston University.

"That house was old, too, and it has a story. Nothing bad happened to us there, but we weren't alone. The house was built by a whaling captain, and years ago, the captain had gone on one too many voyages and failed to return from the last. And every day, his wife would go up to the widow's walk at the top of the house overlooking the harbor hoping he'd come back. But he and his ship had vanished. One evening, my dad was coming up to the house from the harbor at sunset, and he saw her standing over the roof on the widow's walk. She was wearing a black dress with full skirts and staring out to sea. I've wondered if she isn't going to stay there looking until she finds out what happened to him. It's unresolved, and she waits, I supposed. But she never bothered us, not directly."

The dinner table had become very quiet.

Rasputin loped out of the kitchen and headed toward the library. As he left the room the warmth returned.

"Music!" Johnny said.

He cranked the gramophone and soon the sound of Louis Prima chased the shadows away and their good humor returned.

JOHNNY SPENT his Sunday in the library at Silver Beech, examining books and putting them into a sort of order. There was geography, classical history, philosophy, and a myriad of other leather-bound wonders. He was joined by Rasputin, who took up shop in a comfy chair near the fireplace and was busy staring at the shelves across the room from where Johnny was working.

At the moment, Johnny was most intrigued by the Bible he had found. It contained records of a family named Wright and dated back to before the Revolutionary War, which led him to the local public library, hot on the trail of the Wright family, the first thing on Monday morning. Boston could manage a day or two without him, and he thought if he hadn't gone into design, he would have made a marvellous archeologist. Or a detective.

The North Bay Library was many good things: a place to read, research, and even socialize. The Monday morning book group was meeting in the main room, and a group of preschoolers was enjoying story hour in the children's section. The new fiction shelves stood near the checkout desk opposite the front door, and Johnny had to resist the temptation to get lost in a book.

The library staff was happy to help him find out about Silver Beech and quickly led him to an older, quieter, part of the building. The sign said Genealogical Research. There were comfortable wooden work tables and the walls were lined with the portraits of North Bay notables, sea captains, and distinguished gentlemen, some of whom had lived in this building when it was still a residence. The library was almost as old as the village, and here, in the inner sanctum, was a collection of ring binders, one for each house in the village's historic district.

The librarian easily found the file for Silver Beech. Inside was a picture of the house with a small inventory,

according to which the house dated from an original struc-
ture built around 1640. It had undergone many renovations
and additions over the years to become its current example of
the classic Greek Revival style, especially considering the
generous front porch with its wide columns. The file listed
the owners of the house, and there was the name Wright, the
name from the family bible.

The house had been purchased in 1820 by Nathaniel
Wright, but it didn't seem to have been called Silver Beech at
that time. The record said it had stayed in the Wright family
until 1935 when it was bought by Charles Fullerton. Johnny's instincts told him to follow the Wright connection.

"You should really head over to the historical society
across the street to find out more about the Wright family,"
said the librarian. An amateur historian herself, she was
happy to photocopy the house records and point him in the
right direction for the historical society.

"Ask for Tenny Wendell," she said.

LARS SALO SIPPED his second coffee of the day and helped
himself to a donut before returning to his desk at the North
Bay planning department. Planning was a tight enclave
within the local town hall network, and it had a few of its
own traditions. Monday's revolving donut run, for example,
made the start of the week that much brighter.

Lars came from one of the many Finnish families that
had settled on Cape Cod with the brick-making industry in
the 1800s. He was blond and blue-eyed like his mother, and
tall like his dad, and for the last five years, he had lived and
breathed planning because he figured the trick to recovering
from alcohol was to replace the booze with a healthier

option. He'd gone dry after ten years of hard-drinking that had cost him his marriage and his real estate company. When he'd been dry a year, he grabbed the opportunity in the planning department with a laser focus on preserving Cape Cod through careful planning protocol—and preserving himself through clean living.

At 9:00, he was starting to wonder why Sean MacIntosh was not manning the front desk. A little later, his work was interrupted by the bell on the counter, and directing uncharitable thoughts toward Sean, Lars left his desk to find himself lost in a pair of green eyes under a mass of red hair. She was almost as tall as he was, and she looked like a Valkyrie armed with a manila envelope in one hand and a sheet of paper in the other. Her sweater was a comfortable wool cable knit, but her jacket looked like it was from the city.

"The Nickerson land," he heard her say, and the moment passed, and sound returned, and she looked back at him, waiting for an answer.

"The application to clear?" Lars found the very suggestion of clearing that old-growth a travesty.

"Yes, here, I received this in the mail last week. It's addressed to my aunt, but she died recently and left me the house."

Olive handed him the demolition notice.

"You're Eartha's niece?"

"I'm Olive Adams, yes. I want to save the land."

ANN WAS KNEELING on a low tide sand flat half a mile out into the harbor in a pair of old waders. A search of Eartha's barn had revealed a clam rake and basket hanging from a nail next to the waders, and, most fortuitously, an up-to-date shellfishing license attached to the handle of the basket. She checked the tide chart in the kitchen and went straight out to the flats which emerged every low tide behind the marsh at the back of Silver Beech and the Nickerson land.

She was alone with the seagulls, and the wind and the water. She had forgotten the peace of it, the timelessness of it, and the bounty. Each scoop of the long clam rake rendered at least a half dozen littleneck clams. She scooped and filled the basket, and then sat back on her heels and watched the tide coming in. Mindful not to get caught by the water, she began to make her way back to shore.

There were no better chowder ingredients in the world than littlenecks fresh from the harbor, and there was no better place than the quiet, eclectic kitchen at Silver Beech to finally perfect her recipe.

Chapter Five

RASPUTIN THOUGHT the old lady was just another part of the creaky old house he had lived in since he was a kitten and Eartha had found him shivering under the front porch. She let him stay because she needed a mouser, and he didn't remember a time before that. His focus was on warm fires, bird watching, and stalking mice. But he could see the old lady with his keen cat's eyes: she was small, with her hair pinned up, and she wore a long dress. She liked to hang around in high places near the corners of things, and when she did, she would tell Rasputin stories in that way she had of talking directly into his head.

Because he was a cat, Rasputin didn't think there was anything extraordinary about this. It never occurred to him that the other people in the house were any different from the old lady; except the old lady was cold, and as a cat, he would never think of cuddling up next to her on a winter night for a cozy sleep.

The old lady told Rasputin that Eartha was truly gone,

that it was in the natural order of things, and that someday he, too, would go on the same journey. He stared at her as she floated in a corner just below the kitchen ceiling and told him that she was unable to make that journey herself because she still had something to do here in the house—and she needed his help.

He followed her into the library and she asked him to stay there and stare at her as she floated in front of the furthest bookshelf from the desk because she needed someone to see the volume on the shelf behind her. Rasputin sighed and settled in for what might be a long wait.

The North Bay Historical Society was located, appropriately, in an old house near the library, and as a society, it was forever reinventing itself to keep relevant in a quickly changing world. It was a hotbed of relevant exhibits, community events, and, one of the village favorites, volunteers dressed in historic clothes on the front lawn in summer. The lady in the hoop skirts with the parasol had become a popular local fixture.

The building held an extensive collection of village history, and (so far) the lack of climate control hadn't wreaked too much havoc on the pieces. The permanent exhibit was the house itself, decorated in 1800s style with the actual collection. It was a glimpse of old North Bay, and the curator, Tenny Wendell, was on a mission to find out what other treasure was hiding in the many other old houses that lined the historic district. He dreamed of creating revolving temporary displays with this treasure, if only he could find it, to keep the museum fresh and interesting.

Last week the museum had received an unexpected windfall. A well-heeled board member had offered a grant to cover cataloging the contents of local historical houses into itemized books, with the caveat that the items could then be borrowed for temporary exhibits. Tenny named it the Dawson Grant, after the donor Clive Dawson, and was just sitting down to announce the opportunity online when the front door opened and a well-dressed man carrying a notebook walked in. He wondered who on earth would think of using the front door. Most people just came in around the back.

JOHNNY WAS STARTING to wonder if North Bay was stuck in a time warp. Things were old here. Of course, things were old all over New England, but there was a real feeling of age in North Bay, a feeling of time almost stopped. It was palpable at Silver Beech, the library, and now at the historical society. He supposed that made the society's job all the easier.

The sign in front of the museum said open, so he let himself in and found himself in a high ceilinged front hall with flowered wallpaper from the 1940s. The decorator in him wasn't sold on the wallpaper, but he was immediately entranced by the table setting in the adjacent dining room. The linen and silver were gorgeous, and the plates were from the China trade. A three-masted ship sailed through stormy seas above the sideboard and the seats of the mahogany curved-back chairs were covered in worn red velvet. A crystal chandelier lit the table from above. It looked as if a dinner party was about to commence, and the guests would be clad in antebellum evening dress. This sort of living history always got his imagination running, and he was anticipating the evening's menu and the dinner conversation when Tenny Wendell brought him back to the present with a friendly hello.

OLD PETE SPENT the morning in his garden monitoring his pumpkin seeds. He was encouraged to see that not only had they popped, but they were also a good inch taller as a result of the previous night's rain and the warmer temperatures of the last few days. Spring was finally coming.

Pete's garden covered a half acre and was enclosed by a strong fence. Early each spring, he had it rototilled by the teenager down the street because such heroics seemed best left to the young. Then he planted. First the early crops. Peas on their trellis, radishes in their rows, spinach, and lettuce, and as soon as it was warm enough pumpkin seeds. He gave a large area of his garden over to the rambling pumpkin vines, and most years he let the neighborhood kids pick out a few for their jack o' lanterns. But everyone knew the biggest one was his to enter into the annual pumpkin contest.

He thought about Eartha and how they had gardened together for so many years, and he plucked a head of glorious, early Boston lettuce. He would make a salad for lunch, and then perhaps take a nap. But first, he would check up on Rasputin. The cat usually joined him in the garden and was essential for rodent control, but there hadn't been a sign of him over the last couple of days.

Pete crossed the street and, finding no sign of Rasputin outside, let himself into the unlocked back door at Silver Beech, softly calling the cat. The water dish was where it should be in the kitchen, but he didn't find the cat until he entered the library. Rasputin was curled up tight, asleep on a cushioned chair in the corner. The room felt cold, so Pete gave him a blanket from the chest in the living room, and wondering about cat dreams, started home. He was looking forward to his own nap later that afternoon.

Chapter Six

"He's coming in under the Right to Farm Act," Lars said.

"They can raze acres of old-growth on the Nickerson land under a farm act?" Olive said.

She read from the notification:

"What is 'Moraine Land Development'? And who is 'Douglas Dunn'?"

Lars winced. He had clashed with both entities in the past, and Douglas Dunn, who had tripped behind him for years undoing what good he could, was now promoting development of the local landscape for profit. If Lars was doing something, in his personal or professional life, Douglas could be counted on to try to undo it. At times he had succeeded: he was a dangerous adversary, especially when he was in cahoots with Moraine Land Development. Two years ago Douglas and Moriane had teamed up to circumvent local regulations through a series of subterfuges to build Douglas' current house: a McMansion situated too close to the water near the already overburdened harbor. Lars suspected the house was a payoff for the work Douglas had already completed undermining local regulations so Moraine could profit on environmental damage, and he knew this was no time to get into the havoc Dunn had wreaked on his personal life since the two had been boys.

"Moraine is interested in lining its coffers, and land is their major commodity. They'll come in, clear it, build it, and run off with the profit. Green space, preservation, ecosystems, water quality... doesn't matter. They're in it to profit and they don't care. Dougie Dunn is their frontman. He represents them, gets them through town regulations. They're a hard pair to beat," he said. "I know."

Olive put the papers down on the counter and finally looked at the man standing behind it. His sweater brought out the blue in his eyes and he was looking back at her intently. For no reason at all, she grinned. There was nothing funny about the situation they were discussing, but she couldn't help herself. He grinned back, and his blue eyes crinkled.

"But seriously, if you have a minimum of five acres of land and you are going to farm anything—pigs, fruit, vegetables, horses, you name it—if you are going to farm it, you can do a lot of other things as well. Such as clear cut places that should not be clear cut, ostensibly to create your fields." Lars said.

"Pete Souza lives across the street from my aunt's house. He's been there for at least 80 years, and he doesn't think the Nickerson land has ever been touched," Olive said.

"I know Pete. I knew your aunt, too. I'm sorry she's gone," he said.

Olive marveled at how small a town North Bay was. Lars had known she was Eartha's niece when she came in, and Olive reckoned the people of North Bay didn't miss much.

"The Nickerson land has been untouched for a very long time. No one really thought about it, it was just there, even if it is one of the last intact acreages on the Cape. It seems it was held in trust for years and then sold quietly. Moraine bought it. Look, would you like a coffee? The place next door does a great cappuccino."

He couldn't believe he asked, and she couldn't believe she accepted.

By NOONTIME, North Bay Village was buzzing. Maki's, the general store, was filled with landscapers, lawyers, and real estate agents looking for lunch from the plentiful food counter around back. Sandwiches, pizza, hot dogs, the occasional ribs, and a case full of pre-made salads ensured everyone found something, and the cook in Ann was impressed with the options. Especially as she found the one she was looking for: a big steaming kettle of clam chowder held a place of honor on a shelf surrounded by paper cups, napkins, oyster crackers, and salt and pepper shakers. People ladled out their own cupfuls while exchanging earfuls of gossip as she waited for her turn.

Out on the flats that morning, she had decided one way to improve her recipe was to taste as many versions of chowder as she could. If she thought about it, Cape Cod was chowder ground zero, and she remembered the culinary school story about chowder coming to New England with fishermen from France, who made the stew from the seafood they found at hand as they worked, in much the same way bouillabaisse had originated in Marseilles. Variations of chowder existed all along the East coast. You could find chowder with corn in it, chowder made of fish instead of clams, conch chowder in Florida, and in New York, the chowder was tomato-based, no doubt due to the city's Italian cooks. But Ann was a purist, only the most traditional cream base with potatoes would do. When her turn came, she carefully filled her cup; the chowder smelled savory and fresh, with a hint of sage. The sign over the pot read *Cap't Lanson's Chowder*, with a chalk drawing of a grinning littleneck clam and a chef in a white toque holding a big spoon. The lunchtime chowder pot and the people helping themselves from it was a completely normal scene in any Cape Cod village, unremarkable in its mundanity, but it was also a scene you could never find anywhere else.

She sat on the beach and savored her first bite from the plastic spoon they'd given her at the checkout counter. Briny salt, cream, sage, a gentle hint of onion, soft small-cut potatoes. Maybe the sage had been missing in her last working recipe. The breeze was gentle, the sun was warm, and the tide was rising through the marsh grass. It was early enough in the season that the beach was deserted except for a few distant dog walkers. As she looked across the harbor to the lighthouse, she decided that, for now, a chowder was just a chowder, and digging her feet into the warm sand, she realized she didn't need to have a cigarette when she finished.

RASPUTIN WOKE up in a quiet house under a warm blanket. The old lady was still hanging in front of the bookshelf near the ceiling, but his cat's ears told him no one else was home, so he jumped down and started on his regular rounds. He was, after all, the only thing standing between his people and a whole lot of mice they didn't want in the house. The old lady asked him inside his head to come back and stare when the house was full of people again. She sure didn't quit easily.

ANN LEFT the beach rejuvenated and stopped at Maki's again on her way home. She collected celery, onions, potatoes, salt pork, sage, cream, flour, and butter. She tossed in some salad ingredients and a beautiful, crusty baguette. She was grateful to find the house quiet as she unpacked her provisions and found her bearings in the kitchen.

Every cooking implement known to man in the last 50 years was there. She was amazed. It wasn't flash new stuff; rather it was practical equipment that had proved its value and been made to last. A kitchen equipped like that didn't need gimmicky new stuff. She chose a heavy, yellow, oval-shaped Dutch oven and began to render the salt pork on the gas stove.

The smell must have attracted Rasputin. He came and regarded her thoughtfully, and then asked to go outside. The screen door banged shut. She added chopped onions to the pot, stirred them around, then added the celery. She was building a base to receive the clams.

Her littlenecks fought the good fight and were tough to open, but in the end, they were no match for Eartha's old but sharp clam knife in her experienced chef's hands. The littlenecks were shelled and chopped, and their liquor (the water they sat in) was draining through a cheesecloth she was lucky to find in the pantry—because no one wanted grit in their chowder.

When the onions and celery were soft, she sprinkled a decent amount of flour over them, stirred till it was hot, and then added milk. As it thickened she put in chopped potatoes, and then set it to simmer on low heat. When the potatoes were tender, she dropped in the clams and their liquor, stirred, and set the pot to hold on a very low heat for that evening's dinner. She saved the sage for last, thinking it might make an excellent garnish. It was years since she'd been in a kitchen this peaceful, and she felt energized and focused as she went off to soak in the clawfoot tub upstairs.

JOHNNY LAID a fire in the old cookstove in the kitchen against the chilly fog that had descended late that afternoon. It was a thick pea soup sort of fog, the kind that smelled rank like the marsh behind the house.

"Eartha always used to say that in the Cape Cod fog, ghosts have been taken for men, and men have been taken for ghosts," Olive said.

"I can believe it," Johnny said.

They were tucking into Ann's chowder around the big kitchen table. Ann had found some lovely blue willow bowls in the pantry with a set of silver soup spoons. Johnny had made a bouquet of apple blossoms as a centerpiece and decided on an old Louis Armstrong album to chase away any remaining chill. Rasputin had returned and was gauging his chances of snagging some snacks from a perch nearby.

"I thought I had met a ghost earlier today, at the historical society. Olive, have you been there? If I were a ghost, I'd be there. But listen, Olive, I received a kind of job offer from the president of the society this morning, and it involves you and Silver Beech. It's really quite extraordinary," Johnny said.

Olive knew the historical society was active in the village and had even volunteered there as a kid one summer, helping organize parts of the collection. If she were a ghost, she'd be there, too.

"Tenny Wendell is the president of the society. He looks like part of his own exhibit. I ended up there asking for information on the Wright family, following up on the old family bible I found here in the library. Did you know one of the Wrights sailed around the globe by himself in a small three-masted sloop? Tenny dug out an old letter home from a North Bay sea captain harbored in Rio describing how he ran into Wright that far from home! Cape Codders travel!"

"They do, but they usually come home, too. Same in Marblehead," said Ann.

"This chowder's to die for, Ann," Johnny paused to replenish his bowl. "I told Tenny I was doing an inventory of the house here, and he couldn't believe it. He's just announcing a grant the society has come up with for exactly that! Olive, they'll pay me to catalog the historical items in the house if you will agree to let them borrow a selection of their choice for a future exhibit. They're trying to keep the museum relevant and learn more about historic North Bay."

Johnny freshened their wine glasses with the cold chardonnay they had paired with the chowder, and Louis Armstrong finished singing—that was the trouble with gramophones, they stopped.

Olive raised her glass.

"Congratulations Johnny, you're hired," she said. She hadn't been completely comfortable with him cataloging the house as a favor, anyway.

"Marvelous! I'll head to Boston tomorrow afternoon and sort a few things out after I tell Tenny we're on. Then I'll come back and get to work. I think the library is important. So is the Wright family."

Johnny flipped the record and music filled the kitchen again. Rasputin meowed plaintively and headed toward the library.

"He has his digs in the library, have you noticed?" Ann said.

"Keeps me company in there," Johnny said.

Ann passed the salad.

"What did you find out at town hall today, Olive?"

Olive smiled thinking about the impromptu coffee date. The cappuccino and the company had been just about right.

"I ended up meeting with the director of town planning. His name is Lars, and he's big into conservation. But the news isn't good for the Nickerson land. The developer is applying to clear the land as a farm, and that means he can probably get approved. He claims he's going to grow vegetables."

"The Right to Farm Act? That's happened in Marblehead, too. There've been cases where developers apply to clear a farm, and then gradually tack on other things to become something more than a farm that never would have been approved in any historic district to start with. Like the destination wedding and events farm they put up just outside of town. In theory, the farm act is a great thing: it's meant to support small farms, and as a cook, I love to get ingredients from them. I'm absolutely behind the farm to table movement. But there are loopholes, and sometimes things go wrong. My dad goes nuts over it, so I hear a lot about it," said Ann.

"That's what might be happening here, according to Lars, and there isn't much you can do to stop it. They do have to stop clearing a certain distance from the marsh, but it's not enough to save the entire ecosystem that sits there,"

Olive sighed. "The meeting is on Wednesday. I'm meeting Lars there to speak against it. Old Pete and my mother are going, too. Johnny, have you uncovered anything that might help us?"

"Sorry Olive, not yet."

AFTER FIRMING things up with Olive and Tenny over at the historical society, Johnny decided to spend a few hours in the library at Silver Beech before heading back to Boston. He wanted to finish cataloging the last shelf to the left of the fireplace. The final book he examined was a collection of religious essays from 1700. He put on a sweater against the room's chill and was reflecting on how much more serious the reading material was back in the day when Rasputin mewed. The cat had become a permanent fixture in the library.

"What say you, Rasputin—is the devil afoot in New England?" Johnny chuckled and patted the cat. Johnny followed the cat's gaze to the end of the last bookshelf on the right of the mantlepiece. He was going to begin cataloging that section of books when he returned from Boston in a few days.

Rasputin purred, and on an impulse, Johnny went to the shelf and reached for the book the cat seemed so interested in. It was newer than some of the books there, but still old. It was leather-bound and in serious need of neatsfoot oil just like the rest of the collection. He opened it carefully.

"Maisy Hale, Silver Beech, 1892."

The leaves were brittle, but he held it by the spine like an expert, reading the old-fashioned script.

"Olive!" he called. "Olive, come see this!"

She came in from the kitchen where she'd been making coffee, and he handed her the book.

"It's the story of the house."

Rasputin weaved between their legs as he left the library. He was eager to get on with his affairs.

Chapter Seven

The Journal of Maisy Hale

SILVER BEECH, 1892

ON THE NINTH of October in 1820, I arrived in the borning room off the kitchen at Silver Beech. Back then, the house wasn't called Silver Beech, and the borning room, which faced east to welcome the rising sun and new life, had not yet been made into a pantry.

The first thing my father did was name me Mehitable Wright, after some long-forgotten ancestor. Even in 1820, the name was hideously old-fashioned, and I was never actually serious enough to live up to it. So my mother called me Maisy, and that is the name that stuck.

Today I am 72 years old, and I intend to leave an account of the house and what happened here on the night of the 1870 October Gale, and the events leading up to it.

The earliest Wrights arrived from England in the Massachusetts Bay Colony in 1635 in the ship Defense, at a time when the name Mehitable was quite fashionable. You can track the Mehitables through the family bible, which also arrived in the ship *Defense*. Those must have been hard years, with the challenge of building a home, and the constant fear the New England woods seemed to inspire. The Puritans needed a wilderness, and they created it out of the woods of New England. They needed an adversary, so they put the devil there for good measure. At my age, I can be outspoken. There.

My grandfather came down to North Bay from Boston and built this house. He had an eye for the marsh behind it as grazing for his dairy herd and a place to grow cranberries. The oldest part of the house is the massive central chimney around which the house has grown. The house may alter, but the chimney is too big to change, and in a strong wind, it seems to hold the house as an anchor holds a ship.

My father kept the tradition of dairy and cranberries, and we have done well. I was the only child, and a girl, so with my husband I carried on the farm.

I can just remember when the landscape around the house was forest, and not the cleared land of today surrounded by stone walls to keep the sheep safe. It was wilder, with bigger predators that have since vanished, but I never found the devil in the woods. Instead, I found peace. The house offered peace to others as well: to us, and to patriots hiding from tories during the Revolution, which I don't remember, and runaway slaves hiding in the attic on their way north to Canada, which I do remember, and helped to organize.

My mother lived as a creature of the woods, spending as much time as she could outside. My father had a far more pragmatic approach to the natural world: he owned the land and would use it to gain money. I was my mother's child in spirit, and my father's child in law until my marriage.

There came a time when my mother died, and my father

granted her last wish. As much as he cleared the land of forest, and at the time, land was easy to come by and we owned large swathes of it, he would leave her favorite part untouched: the land directly adjacent to our house and the surrounding gardens, from the path in front to the marsh and the ocean behind. That piece of land numbered 15-acres and held an almost spiritual significance for her, and so he promised and lived to keep his promise. In my turn, I spent many happy hours wandering there at peace, as my mother had before me, and there I felt close to her. We called it my mother's portion.

There came the time of my marriage. I married a farmer's son, one who could manage the land when my father grew too old. Matthew Hale was a progressive thinker, a man planning the future with a Harvard education behind him, for all that he came from a farm and knew how to manage one. And he managed it well, and he left my mother's promised portion untouched as more and more trees were felled to make fields.

There came the birth of my twin sons. They were the last to arrive in the old borning room; we have since used the space as a pantry for the kitchen. They were born in the morning on the first of June, 1845, first Matthew, who we named for his father, and then Thomas, who we named for my father. The addition of Thomas was a surprise to us all, but we were blessed with two sons. They were not identical. Thomas had a head full of dark hair, and young Matthew was blond like I am.

My boys were inseparable. They grew strong, and in time, went to the schoolhouse by the church and received the rudiments of education. They ranged far and wide through fields and woods, and sailed and fished the harbor. They learned to hunt and keep the cattle and grow the cranberries and were partners in all they did. When they were old enough, they followed their father to Harvard, and finally came home to farm.

On their first birthday, I planted two silver beech trees before the house, a sapling for each twin, to celebrate their survival of the dangerous first year of life. More babies died than lived to age one, and I felt now the way ahead was safe and clear for them. The trees were a celebration, and they grew as the boys did. Eventually, the house came to be known as Silver Beech in honor of the trees before it.

And all that time, my mother's land stood untouched, and that was what came between my boys.

It seems my Matthew has been dead for an awfully long time. He died of a fever in '65, the year the war between the states ended. He was fine that morning and gone that evening, and the land went to my boys. We buried my Matthew quickly in the churchyard on the hill overlooking the harbor. We didn't want the fever to spread, and it didn't. It took only him.

The land went to the boys. Both my boys knew about my father's promise to keep my mother's portion untouched, and both had ranged it as boys as it grew thicker and ever more wild. And all around us, the land was being cleared to accommodate the sheep, which were easy to graze on land that was hard to farm. Each sheep field cleared felled more trees, and each field cleared was surrounded by walls made from stones painfully prized from the reluctant earth to mark their boundaries and keep the sheep in. It was a painful reshaping of the landscape, and Thomas truly saw the future in sheep and wanted to clear my mother's portion and give it over to livestock for the profit he could glean from it, but young Matthew wouldn't hear of it. He was determined the land should remain untouched as it always had and has their grandfather promised.

"What use is an old promise? They're both long dead, and none the wiser! It's pure profit. Look around you. We don't need the woods, we need fields and sheep!" Thomas said.

And young Matthew refused to budge.

"The farm is viable as it is. We don't need more fields, and what about the game there? I've brought out plenty of fat deer for the table, and what about the quiet? Where else can you escape the bleating sheep and the sawmill sawing and the axes ringing?"

According to their father's will, both boys must be in agreement before any big decision was made. And so the impasse grew, and Thomas's frustration knew no bounds, and I grieved to see my boys divided.

And there came the time of the October Gale in 1870. The day dawned dim and gray, without sunshine, but we didn't think much about it at first. October is often gray after all, and the beech trees in front of the house were shedding their leaves for the cold season as usual. In 1870, I was 52 years old, but I didn't yet feel the years as I do now, and both my sons were young and strong and still at home.

By midday, the breeze had begun to pick up. Thomas came in looking for young Matthew. He told me he had bought 200 head of sheep for a song. They needed grazing space, and he must clear my mother's portion now as there would be no other place to put them once they arrived the following spring. If the land was going to be ready to graze with new growth in time they needed to cut the trees and pull the bigger rocks immediately before the frost set in.

The wind moaned gently in the trees outside.

We caught a glimpse of Matthew through the window, heading into my mother's portion with his fishing rod. He must have been going to cast a few in the marshy creek beyond the trees. The darkening sky and rising wind were not unheard of in October, but I felt an extra chill beneath them. I shivered, but the *moment passed as Thomas grabbed his coat and started after his brother.*

That was the last time I saw them.

An hour later, the sky had darkened to night, though evening was still far off. The wind screamed in from the northeast, driving heavy rain and hail before it. The trees keened, and the air filled with debris and branches ripped from the wind-whipped trunks. It was a terrifying gale, and it was coming in on a full high tide. All I could do was stay well away from the windows after the first one shattered in the dining room.

I waited with the cat, otherwise, the house was empty. We heard the silver beech to the right of the front door crack. It was a loud death crack. The wind carried the top of the tree away from the house to the field across the street. I had always thought of that tree as young Matthew's tree, and it was Matthew's body we found after the storm, under another tree on mother's portion. We never found a trace of Thomas at all.

The storm was so severe that many towns flooded and villages lost whole fishing fleets that couldn't make it to harbor in time. Many lives were lost that day in North Bay and on Cape Cod, my boys among them.

And so came the time of my waiting. I buried Matthew with his father and set to wait for news of Thomas, and now I am 72 years old.

When my time comes, I have arranged to leave the farm to my cousin, Nathaniel Nickerson, in Connecticut, with the provision that he return it to Thomas if Thomas should ever come home. Thomas has been gone long enough for the law to assume he is dead, but in my mother's heart, I know he lives. The other provision in my will is that mother's portion be protected from clearing in perpetuity and that it be called the Nickerson land, after Nathaniel and his line. In my mind, this will save the land as promised, in memory of my mother, and also of my son, Matthew. And perhaps renaming the land will cleanse it of its bad memories and bring it and me peace.

And so I wait for news of Thomas, and I keep the land intact. I will leave this account in the library with my family bible that it may tell the story of Silver Beech, and a promise kept, and my boys, and especially the story of my endless wait.

Maisy Hale

Chapter Eight

MIA NICKERSON WAS FURIOUS. The ongoing drought, the gunmetal heat, the rain that never relieved the parched California landscape threatened by fire, and now her brother's most recent real estate caper were enough to ruin anyone's morning. There was not enough coffee in the world for this one.

"But we're getting top price selling out to Moraine Development, and they've got a local guy who can get through the regulatory boards," said Nate.

"Let me get this straight. You're over-leveraged on your ski condo, your sports car, your second divorce settlement, and I don't know what else, and you think selling that parcel of land on Cape Cod will solve your problems? What are you planning to sell when the next round of bills hit?"

"Mia, I've already signed the papers. Your 45 percent is on the way." She slammed down the phone and stared at the brown landscape outside her office window.

New England has a long tradition of public meetings designed to air everyone's opinions and ultimately arrive at the fair consensus of a matter, and the North Bay Preservation Society was no different. The society's stated goal was to uphold the historical integrity of the village. It regulated architecture, paint color, and signage to ensure the village retained its history and charm, and it was part of a larger network of societies across the Cape and islands committed to the same goal. The parts of Cape Cod that had preserved their visual history had done so largely due to the efforts of such groups.

On a Wednesday evening in late June, the volunteer board of the North Bay Preservation Society discovered it was not able to approve outright the motion to clear cut the Nickerson land as Douglas Dunn sat spitting nails across the table from his old adversary in love, life, and land management, Lars Salo.

Peter Souza opened the meeting by extolling the pristine condition of the land and the lack of any precedent for clearing it. He suggested the proposed farm scale back its plan to a more sustainable model.

Lars considered the environmental impact of cutting on the landscape outlining the role of the trees in absorbing water: no trees could mean flooding. He highlighted the endangered species act: what was living there that needed to be protected? He advised caution in the application of zoning laws that offered loopholes, such as the Right to Farm Act currently under discussion.

Olive and Rose spoke as neighbors who generally supported farms, but suggested a smaller plan allowing a healthy buffer of the mature forest to remain so the ecosystem could have some protection. Together Olive, Rose, and Pete expressed their shared concern that the increased traffic and activity the farm might attract could put the land under even more pressure, and that clear-cutting 15-acres would cause unsightly and irreversible damage to the landscape.

Douglas Dunn, clad in a shiny black sports coat with pointed black shoes, brushed bits of loose tobacco from his lapel. His black hair was oiled straight back and the smell of Axe cologne preceded him as he rose to make the simple, compelling case that his client, Moraine Development, was completely within its rights under the Right to Farm Act to clear the land for the proposed farm. There was really no reason to deny the application. His confidence was palpable.

Finally, Olive held up the old journal Johnny had found in Eartha's house, and claimed that, if anything, it showed a precedent for keeping the land just as it was. She passed out photocopies of Maisy Hale's account as she told the story, and the North Bay Preservation Society listened, rapt with interest. Even though they had all been friends of Eartha's and Rose had grown up with one of them, the story in the journal came as a complete surprise. Old Pete broke the silence at the end of the tale and said it was a surprise to him as well, and he'd been living right there his whole life.

The board voted unanimously to continue the application for one month to allow further information to be gathered on all aspects of the proposed clearing.

Douglas Dunn was furious, but he had an answer prepared. It worked every time.

"If you're really serious about saving the land, you certainly can. But you'll need to buy it from Moraine Development on their terms," he said with hard eyes and hard smile.

He thrust a business card into each of their hands.

"Contact me here if you're interested. Otherwise, I'll see

you here at the next meeting, with a lawyer who can certainly remind us of how the Farm Act works." Olive thought he wasn't called The Axe for nothing as he turned on his heel and strode from the room.

As the meeting broke up, Douglas Dunn watched the others leave from his car at the very back of the parking lot. He kept a strict policy to never park out in the open, because the less people saw of him the better. He ground a cigarette into the ashtray behind closed windows in the smoke filled car as the last strains of vintage heavy metal faded from the speakers. He gently started his engine as Lars and Olive pulled into the main road, and as he gently pressed the gas he felt the hatred he had harbored over the years for Lars build. From their earliest days, it was always Lars being chosen to captain sports teams, it was always Lars out-sailing him in summer regattas, Lars had been homecoming king their senior year, it had been Lars dating Jean, his would have been, could have been love if only not for Lars. Douglas's other strict policy was to undermine everything Lars did, and he had been surprised to find it profitable when Lars went into land preservation and he obviously went into land development. He savored the hatred and pulled into the street at a discreet distance from Lars' motorbike behind Olive's car.

LATER THAT EVENING, Lars regarded Olive across a candlelit table at the Sea Urchin. One of North Bay's oldest and most popular watering holes, the Sea Urchin sported a popular bar and a traditional but hopping dining room. It was a place to meet, greet, and maybe snag a quiet table.

Lars had suggested the quiet table option in the wake

of the meeting. He had certainly had his times at the Sea Urchin when he was drinking, and he didn't often return to the scene, so to speak, but this felt different. Maybe now he was ready to socialize again, this time with a clearer head.

"Talk about historic preservation! I'll bet this place hasn't changed in fifty years!" said Olive.

Just getting in the door and through the bar, they'd had to stop and greet most of the people there. Olive found that Lars was a popular figure in the village and stopped trying to remember all the new names. It was a friendly bunch, and the bar was crowded for mid-week, but the dining room was quiet. They were just in time to order something before the kitchen closed.

"Definitely the chowder," Olive said. She had adopted Ann's mission and was now committed to tasting the local chowder variations.

Lars noticed how the candlelight played with the highlights in Olive's hair. She had certainly turned more than a few heads passing through the bar.

"Were you named Olive for your green eyes?" he said.

It was the oldest line in the book, but coming from him it sounded different.

"Yes," she said.

Lars cleared his throat. For a moment, he was completely lost for words.

"Let's eat Cape Cod. The chowder, and stuffed quahogs!" he said.

Stuffed quahogs are a uniquely Cape Cod creation, and the Sea Urchin made the best. The meat of a large, hard-shelled clam was mixed into chorizo, onion, herb, and butter stuffing and re-stuffed into the quahog shell. Popped under a

Mary Petiet

hot broiler, it came out crispy on the outside and a tiny bit gooey on the inside.

They could smell the marsh behind the restaurant, and then someone behind the bar played the piña colada song with its line about the 'dunes on the cape,' and Olive recognized the moment as both completely authentic and totally clichéd. It wasn't a bad way to end an evening after an inconclusive meeting.

Douglas parked across the street from the Urchin and ambled up to Lars' motorbike. He paused, lit a cigarette, fumbled, and dropped his lighter. As he stooped to find it, he let most of the air out of the bike's front tire. Rising, he resumed his smoke and stood a minute before approaching the screened-in back door of the restaurant kitchen. As he expected, his old friend Don was there washing dishes. He motioned to him and slipped a fifty through the door.

"Jean in there?" He asked.

"Yeah," Don grunted, wet with dishwater, soap, and food.

"Use this," he showed the money, "and get her well juiced up." Don smelled cheap cologne over the regular kitchen smells.

"She already *is* well juiced up, " Don said doubtfully.

Douglas slipped him another fifty.

"Say it's on the house."

Don sighed, his inner battle for good overcome by the pressure he was under to pay a pile of bills.

Douglas smiled coldly and walked back to his car. His mother had chosen his name because she liked it. She hadn't understood it meant dark horse, and in so naming him she was invoking all that was dark in North Bay.

THE CHOWDER ARRIVED first and smelled delicious. Olive put Douglas Dunn's business card on the table between them before picking up her spoon.

"What do you think?"

"He's tried it before. He's banking on the opposition being unable to find the funds. Usually, they can't," answered Lars, thoughtfully. "It's worked before, too."

She tasted the chowder. It was perfect. She'd have to tell Ann.

"Tell me about the journal, how did you turn that up at just the right time?" he asked.

"That's the funny thing. We needed it and it was there."

He listened to the story of Johnny and the cataloging job for the historical society and was impressed by how many people were actively working to save local history despite the effort of the developers.

"It's probably not enough," he said.

The unspoken question was how to raise the needed funds in the short amount of time they had.

"We need to approach organizations that preserve land and habitats. We don't have a lot of time," Olive said.

Suddenly they heard a harsh laugh and Lars looked up toward the bar.

"Would you look at that!"

A blonde woman in a leather jacket was pointing at them.

"Jean, don't," said a voice behind her. Don was clearing

glasses and becoming more uncomfortable with the situation every moment. There was no sign of Douglas.

"Don't what? Who's the chick, Lars?" she sneered.

The charm of the previous moment was broken, and Olive felt things spinning out of control.

Lars stood up, he knew there was no reasoning with Jean in this state.

"Who is she, Lars?" Jean mocked.

People were starting to notice.

"Lars, look, I've got to go," Olive rose quietly from her seat. "I'm not sure what's going on here, but it's not about me."

Together, they made for the front door. Lars opened it and followed her out. Neither of them noticed Douglas' car parked across the street.

Jean's laughter echoed behind them.

"Don't say anything, Lars. Just don't," Olive said, glad she'd brought her own car and furious with herself for imagining a future with him.

Lars watched her go and wondered when his past would rest. He started his motorcycle. If he could go fast enough he might outrun his demons.

THE NEXT MORNING found Old Pete watering his pumpkin plants. His seeds had sprouted and were fast becoming vines. As Pete worked, Rasputin turned up to play a bit in the sprinkler, for he was one of those odd cats that like water. Pete told him to have a mind towards rodents. They tended to become emboldened by the heat and had decimated the garden more times than Pete liked to remember, like the time he had gone out fishing and left a row of beans on the vine that had just reached their peak. He had looked forward to them all day, and when he returned to pick them, they were gone. The poles they had grown on were ruined, the roots were exposed, and not a bean remained. That night he ate fresh bluefish with no beans.

Rasputin made his way back to Silver Beech the long way: across the street and through the shade of the Nickerson land. He was about to meow at the back door when he heard the clatter of a dropped coffee cup as the radio announced a motorcycle crash that had happened overnight in North Bay.

Chapter Nine

THERE WAS a tradition in the Nickerson family that a certain piece of land on Cape Cod remain untouched in the family trust. Mia and Nate had never seen this land in person, but that did not diminish its role in the family mythology. According to their grandfather, his grandfather, Nathaniel, had inherited a farm from a distant cousin on Cape Cod around the year 1900. It consisted of a beautiful farmhouse and acreage, and the Nickersons had rented it out to tenants for many years, always with the provision that the adjoining woodland remain untouched. That had been the stipulation in the will, and they had always abided by it.

By the time Nathaniel had inherited the Cape land, his son Harding had been in California for at least twenty years. He had originally gone west for easier farming (nothing was harder than trying to coax crops from the reluctant New England soil), but he had quickly fallen into the frenzy of the Gold Rush. Harding found a business partner who had come from New England as well, on a clipper out of Boston, and the two had begun amassing a fortune—not in mining, as one would imagine, but in providing equipment to the miners. There was big profit to be had selling shovels, sifters, brushes, heavy equipment, coffee beans and salt pork, and all manner of supplies that eluded most of the fortune hunters who were blinded by gold. The family liked to joke that he had failed to contract gold fever and thus succeeded. Harding's business partner was Thomas Smith, and when Harding married Thomas's daughter Felicity, two family fortunes became one.

As the gold rush subsided, the partners pivoted to real estate and continued to build their assets, until they became old men and handed the reins over to their sons. Thomas, usually a quiet man, had become quite talkative on his deathbed, and surprised them all with an old secret: His last name was Hale, and he had fled to California from Cape Cod as an apparent fugitive.

There had been a fight with his brother over a piece of land, there had been a storm, and when his brother had died beneath a storm-felled tree, he had blamed himself and fled on the first ship out of Boston. The land in question was the same woodland that adjoined the Nickerson house on Cape Cod. It was his childhood home, in fact, with the marriage of Felicity and Harding, the two families had but been rejoined. He grieved for his long-dead mother, and his brother, and told them the adjoining woodland, the Nickerson land, must always remain untouched. It was all he could do now in their memory.

And the Nickersons had always kept the promise. In 1935, as their fortunes waned with the depression, Mia and Nate's grandfather, Jared, had sold the house and surrounding acreage on Cape Cod to a family named Fullerton. At that time, Jared separated the woodland, called the

Nickerson land, into a trust in the name of his grandchildren, and because he was an old-fashioned man he had given his grandson Nate the controlling interest, and this proved to be the undoing of a long tradition.

Mia supposed most families had stories, traditions, odd coincidences, and more than a few secrets. She usually didn't spend much time thinking about theirs, she was too busy working in conservation. The past had been about selling land and developing it, but her present was about protecting land and rewilding it, and she only needed to look out her office window at the parched, fire-prone landscape to remind herself why.

Her office walls at Save the Land were covered with maps that showed each piece of land the non-profit had conserved. Save the Land's goal was to outbid, outbuy, and out finance the developers causing the destruction. They did this through a combination of fundraising and donations, and the more the public understood what was at stake, the more support they received. Donations seemed to climb in the wake of severe weather and fire as if people might be heeding the alarm sent out by a planet under siege.

"Mia, stop it with the tree hugger stuff. No one remembers why the Nickerson land is undeveloped, and it's serving no purpose just sitting there," Nate told her over the phone the week after she had received her share of the proceeds.

She didn't know what to do with the money. It didn't seem like it was rightly hers, and she was disgusted by the whole situation.

"Wrong, Nate. *We* remember, and *we* know," she said.

OLD PETE CAME over to Silver Beech with a bunch of fresh sage and thyme from his garden. He was looking for Ann with thoughts of her developing chowder recipe. Rasputin was two steps ahead of him, as usual. He found the cat at the screen door on the porch and gave a gentle knock.

"Pete, have you heard about Lars? It has to be Lars. The news said there was a motorcycle accident last night, a speeding driver didn't make a corner on Main Street." Pete read the anxiety on Olive's face as she held the door open for him. In her mind's eye, she saw Lars mounting his bike in the parking lot of the Urchin.

Her cell phone rang.

"Excuse me, Pete."

Pete watched her eyes grow wide as she listened. Rasputin wove between them as Pete gave his tail a gentle tug.

She put the phone down.

"That was my mother. She and dad have some way of listening in on emergency transmissions. A police scanner thing. She said it was Lars in the crash. Only thing wrong with the bike was a flat tire that probably caused a spin-out. He's at the hospital in Hyannis. He's in bad shape," Olive said, in disbelief. "And I was just at the Sea Urchin with him last night!"

She told Pete what had happened, and he nodded sagely as he pulled out a chair at the table for Olive before taking his own seat.

"I've known Lars Salo his whole life. He comes from a good family. He's a good man. But about ten years ago, he got into trouble. Drinking too much. He was married to his high school sweetheart, that's Jean you saw at the bar last night, and they were hanging around with a rough bunch, drinking most of the time. Lars lost his business because of the drinking. At the last minute, about five years ago, he quit booze. Just like that. I think that saved his life. He quit drinking, and Jean didn't. They've been divorced for three years, he's had a long hard crawl back, and he made it. The Lars you know is older and wiser for his past, and the only thing he kept from his bad old days was that damned motorcycle," said Pete.

Douglas Dunn sat at his desk enjoying the ocean view from his office in the big house on the water which occupied a significant part of the North Bay harbor waterfront. The sun was climbing the sky and the whale watch boat was heading out on the calm waters of a half-tide laden with sunburned tourists. Douglas smiled recalling Lars' pained opposition to building the big house as he rammed through a series of zoning application meetings to obtain local permission and then swiveled in his chair to regard the map of the Nickerson land covering the wall behind his desk. The office and the big house were quiet outposts of Moraine Land Development, where Douglas Dunn lived and worked as their local man on the ground, and as he stuck pins in the map to plot the first incursion of clearing machinery, his phone rang.

"You hear the news? Lars crashed his bike last night," Don from the Urchin announced.

Douglas drank it in.

"You there?"

"Yeah. I got a meeting."

"Lars is non-responsive in the ER."

"I gotta go," Douglas said. As far as he knew, no one had

seen him near the bike or even at the Urchin, except Don, and Don wasn't going to talk.

THE ANIMALS SLUNK deeper and deeper into the woods as the men came closer. Their heavy boots were loud and they talked in rough voices as they navigated through the thickets and trees.

"Damned thick growth, watch the poison ivy!"

"Ever seen so many mosquitoes? We gotta drain this swamp."

Moraine had a strict policy to never hire local surveyors or land clearing companies, so the men were from Boston with no known ties to the Cape. To them, it was just another piece of land to clear, all in a days work.

The animals slipped deeper into the trees, sensing the surveyor's ill intention. The path behind them was fluttered with pink ribbons as they marked the first trees marked for cutting and wooden stakes they planted intermittently to show the straightest possible route to follow from the main road clear to the marsh. Birds swarmed overhead watching while the trees murmured warning on the gathering breeze.

JOHNNY PULLED in under the beech tree about an hour later in the old brown delivery van. He had sorted out his Boston business for the time being, and he was eager to continue cataloging. He had put the word out on Beacon Hill that he was going down to the Cape on a buying expedition between renovation jobs, so he would need to find some yard sale treasure to add just the right shabby chic texture to a few houses he could think of. He hadn't even had a chance to read Maisy's journal yet and was anxious to get his hands on it.

The day was sunny and warm, and the house was deserted but for the cat. He found the journal on the kitchen table in a pile of papers from the town meeting, cleaned up the broken coffee cup he found on the floor and began to read in a shady spot on the porch. Soon enough, he grabbed the big old family bible from the library and began to compare the names in the journal to the names in the bible, and they squared perfectly. Marvelous! He knew how rare it was for research to match up so well, and while he couldn't wait to tell Tenny at the historical society, he decided to let Olive in on it first.

Rasputin mewed and stared up toward the porch ceiling. The old lady was hanging there watching Johnny read, and she told Rasputin in her quiet way that he'd done such a good job pointing out the book.

JEAN WOKE up at lunchtime with an ashtray mouth and a metaphorical ax through her forehead. Maybe the stuff really is poison, she thought. How many beers? Then the regret settled in, almost comfortable, almost an old friend, and she remembered Lars' face as she mocked him and the redhead, and she heard again the voice behind her saying, "No, Jean, don't."

What had she done? Something felt wrong. She sat up in bed and felt nauseous, and finally made it to the kitchen door where someone had been pounding for quite some time.

Her friend Max Loring stood there and he looked scared.

"Lars wiped out his bike last night. He's in intensive. Not sure how bad, but bad," he said in a rush.

He thought Jean looked awful.

"Don from the kitchen sent you home last night in an Uber. You alright?"

"No, Max, I'm not alright," Jean sat down as the regret flowed over her and she wondered how she could fix it all.

"It's my fault, Max. I need to clear my head, I need to stop drinking. I need to talk to Lars."

"Can't nobody talk to him now, he can't hear."

Jean sighed heavily and looked out the window at the blindingly bright day. The trees were full of chattering squirrels and the sky was alive with birds.

"Max, will you take me in to East House? Drive me there and drop me off?"

Max gaped.

East House was the local rehabilitation hospital for substance abusers. The disturbing underbelly of Cape Cod's unique beauty was perhaps the pervasive problem of addiction and the spiritual and material poverty that came with it. Alcohol was no stranger to the locals, and more recently, opioids had come in hard on the heels of alcohol. Very few families remained unscathed by one or the other, and this morning something in Jean could see what she had to fix, for herself and the people she cared about.

"I need to clear my head, Max. I need to fix this. I'll check myself in—I want to go now, and I just need a ride. I need to change this," she gestured to herself and her squalid apartment, the bottles on the table.

"I need to fix things for Lars," she said.

LARS WAS FLOATING and looking down: he could see everything he knew in microcosm. He saw his favorite part of the marsh, with the swell of the ocean beyond, and fields and stonewalls and coyotes and deer. He saw himself with Jean back when they'd been a golden couple, just out of school with the world before them. She held on tight to his waist as they rode his bike into Ptown on a warm summer day, her hair streaming blonde behind her. He saw his parents and his favorite dog, and himself hitting a home run. He smelled his mother's apple pie, felt the swoop of his sailboat heeling before a brisk wind, and he saw Jean riding his bike alone, and he saw a pair of green eyes under a cloud of red hair, and he floated and was content.

Chapter Ten

IT WAS LUNCHTIME, and Ann was eating chowder in Dennis. She had decided to try the chowder in each of the Cape's towns to narrow down the best attributes of each and then combine them as her own. The North Bay chowder was thick and potato-ey, but this Dennis chowder was thinner and soupier. Consistency was important, she reflected and chuckled as she recalled the rumors at culinary school of overwhelmed cooks dumping mashed potato powder into their chowder pots in desperate bids for instant thickening. Another bite and she thought the thinner broth might amplify the herbs. This one had sage and thyme. It was delicious. They all were. She hadn't had a bad one yet.

She was sitting in the afternoon sun on the breakwater at Sesuit Harbor watching the boats. Sailboats tacked their way out, weaving between Boston Whalers and bigger fishing boats. There were plenty of kids out having a great time, and she watched a whole line of ten-year-olds navigate their small Opti sailing dinghies from the Dennis Yacht Club out past the breakwater to sail in a mock race off the beach. The breeze was cool and just right, there was not a cloud in the sky, and she threw away her last cigarettes with her empty chowder cup.

OLIVE FOUGHT to focus on the road as she drove to the hospital with Pete. If only she'd let Lars speak before they parted last night. If only she'd given him a chance to explain the situation. She had just assumed the worst and left in a huff.

"This is my fault," she said.

"Don't be ridiculous and don't beat yourself up. Last night was about a whole bunch of things you just walked into, and Lars didn't have time to explain."

"I didn't give him the time!"

"You couldn't have known."

"You CAN'T SEE HIM," said the ER nurse.

"His parents are with him now. He's taken a serious blow to the head despite the helmet. In fact, the helmet cracked open when it hit the tree. He isn't conscious, and I'm not sure if he knows his parents are there. There isn't much you can do but wait."

So they waited, and eventually, a woman with short gray hair wearing a pair of jeans with a long-sleeved peasant blouse and white clogs came out of the room. Pete greeted her like an old friend.

"Elea, this is Olive Fullerton," he said.

"I'm so sorry, Mrs. Salo," said Olive.

"We think Olive was the last person to see Lars before his accident," said Peter.

ANN HAULED her peck of littlenecks off the low tide flats late that afternoon, content in the lowering sun. The tide was lapping its way in, and with it came the working boats of the oyster farmers, sturdy Carolina skiffs that could navigate in almost no water at all, while from the shore, sailboats began to launch into the rising water. The wind was from the southwest, the air was soft, and she was planning what to put into this particular batch of chowder.

As she walked up from the marsh through the Nickerson land, the creek and marshgrass slowly gave way to trees. A surprised flock of ducks rose as she passed and she was surrounded by the sounds of nature. This was one of the few spots left on the Cape where silence reigned, with no background hum of traffic; unless an airplane flew overhead, all was birdsong and insects and wind through the tall trees.

She was looking forward to Pete's herbs. They had agreed the day before that he would supply as many chowder ingredients as he grew in his garden. She was aiming to make it as local a creation as she could, and between her own clamming expeditions and Pete's contributions, it was coming together well. One thing she didn't think she could get locally was salt pork. She was working on that one.

She put her littlenecks in the big soapstone sink to soak and discovered a large bunch of sage and thyme on the kitchen table. She found Johnny transfixed by a pile of books in the library.

"I need a breather. Iced tea?" he said.

They sat on the shady porch. Johnny's Nantucket red chinos went perfectly with his loafers, which he wore without socks as a concession to the warm weather. His white polo shirt was casually untucked, and he pushed back his bangs which were falling just so. It always took him a moment to return to the present when he'd been immersed in the past.

"If you stay here long enough you might forget the modern world altogether. Do you know that old musical, *Brigadoon*? It's kind of like that: when the hunters stumble upon the old Scottish town that only shows itself once a year and has never changed. This house feels enchanted that way, too," he said.

"Usually it's ghosts who are trapped in the past, not houses," said Ann.

"Once, when I was growing up in Marblehead, I looked up into the second-floor window of a big old Victorian house. Something had caught my eye. I saw a figure there, moving around, wearing old-fashioned clothes. I was too young to be polite, so I pointed up and asked 'Who's that upstairs?' As far as I knew, everyone was outside on the lawn where my parents were visiting with the people who lived there. My mother's friend said it was Delphinia: 'Lots of people have seen her. In the late 1800s, her baby died in the old nursery. We use the nursery today as a linen closet, but Delphinia is still there, looking for her baby. Sometimes she even tears all my neat shelves apart. Want to see?' Off we went to see, but everything seemed quiet. 'Sometimes when I'm brushing my hair in the mirror I see another woman's face there as well. I think it's Delphina. And sometimes we hear a game of cards but can't seem to find out where in the house it's taking place,' my mother's friend told me. Most of these stories have one thing in common: the house is the backdrop for the action. The house has changed through time, but the ghosts don't realize it and are stuck there for some reason, repeating scenes that happened long ago."

"Silver Beech might be the reverse situation," said Johnny. He shivered. "Someone's sure walking on my grave!"

"Maybe the land remembers. I felt like that walking up the Nickerson land from the marsh just now."

They looked out at the tangled trees next door, both feeling the wildness of it. Behind the woods, the sunset streaked the western sky scarlet.

"Red sun at night, sailor's delight," said Ann.

"Let's make that chowder," said Johnny.

THE DAY HAD PASSED while Olive and Pete waited in the quiet, air-conditioned hospital, but they hadn't really felt the passage of time. Olive often thought time ceased to exist altogether in airports and hospitals, and she was surprised to realize the day was fading and she was hungry. There had been no change in Lars's condition. He was stable, but he wasn't waking up, and they couldn't tell the extent of the damage to his brain until he regained consciousness.

His parents were gracious. Her account of the previous evening had given the story some perspective, and they warmed up a bit when they realized she was Eartha's niece. She had kept apologizing, but Elea truly didn't blame her.

"Lars mentioned you the last time I saw him. You're trying to save the Nickerson land. It's Lars's cause now, too. He spoke highly of you. I'm happy to meet you, but I'm sorry about the circumstances."

Olive was impressed, but she wondered if the reality of the situation had hit Elea yet. She was almost too composed.

"Lars'll come out of this, you'll see. He's been in worse

shape before. Well, almost," said Lars's father Kurt. He had a nice smile and his hands were marked by a lifetime of labor.

Neither parent had strayed far from the bedside all day. Olive and Pete could only imagine what they were going through.

The doctor reported late that afternoon that they would simply have to wait. Everything that could be done had been done.

"You and Pete should head home and get some rest. We'll call right away if there is any change," Elea promised.

"Johnny, can you mince up the sage and the thyme for me please?" Ann's hands were busy shucking the littlenecks. She was tanned by the sun, and her hair had begun to grow out.

The gramophone was playing the blues, and Johnny had set a special table with a hosta leaf at each place to hold the soup spoon. Ann was always amazed by the ideas Johnny came up with to create a whimsical scene. She remembered she needed to check in on the restaurant, and that made her think he might do a world of good to the dining room at The Quahog Connection.

"My mother puts dill in her chowder," Johnny said.

Dill. That was a thought.

"Ok, next time let's try dill. Have you noticed Pete's garden? It's huge. It's a small farm. But notice how it settles into the landscape. It's part of the larger organic whole. And there is plenty of dill there, too. A farm can be had without destroying the landscape. Pete's is proof."

"Mom uses red potatoes. Not yukons."

He flipped the record and lit the candles while Ann stirred the chowder pot.

"Actually, I think she adds sherry. It must be sherry."

Ann put the chopped littlenecks into the pot.

"Mom uses sea clams, not littlenecks."

She wondered where on the flats she might find sea clams, finished stirring in the littlenecks, and reached for the cream.

"Mom uses milk, never cream."

Johnny laughed, poured them each a cold pinot grigio, and clicked his glass against hers.

"To first place, *Boston's Best!*" he said.

The screen door bumped open, and Pete and Olive walked in with Rasputin at their heels.

"There you are! We're making chowder," Ann said.

"I CAN'T BELIEVE you went the whole day without hearing anything about Lars," said Olive.

It's true, Ann thought wryly, time does stop in this house. She ladled out chowder and Johnny dressed the salad.

Olive had found it comforting to arrive home—she was thinking of it as home now, she noticed—to a warm kitchen full of friends, music, and the rich smell of chowder. It was the exact opposite of the hospital's clinical sterility and having explained the situation, she tried not to dwell on where Lars was now. If only she could turn the clock back to this time last night, if only he were here eating chowder with them all. The longer Lars lay silent in his hospital bed the more he seemed to speak in her heart.

"Since there is nothing you can do at this exact moment for Lars, I have an idea," Johnny announced. He had been thinking about this since his last trip to Boston. It might be a solution to the Nickerson land.

"A lot of research and preservation comes down to grant money. Think of how Tenny over at the historical society hired me with a grant. Very few individuals have the required finances, and the arts, research, and preservation projects are always under siege, so nonprofits and grants often fill the gap. Maybe there is a grant that would save the Nickerson land. Maybe that's how you could patch together the money you need to buy out the developer."

It was an excellent idea.

"See if there's one for the development of clam chowder," Ann said.

"The chowder's marvelous, Ann," said Johnny.

Olive thought she must have some contacts from her magazine days who might be able to help find leads on grants and wondered how she hadn't thought of it herself. While she waited for Lars to wake up she would apply to every grant she could find. She hoped she would have wonderful news for him when the time came.

JEAN'S ENTRY to East House was harrowing. She was lucky to get a bed, and once she started to feel marginally better she immediately wanted a drink. Only now she couldn't have one. The doctors had made sure she was hydrated, and as the detox settled in, she found herself fighting all her demons in addition to the insane, shaking cravings for booze. She saw wild things: Lars was young again and playing on the football team, and she was young again and hadn't ever had a drink, and Douglas Dunn was trying to keep up with them both and falling ever further behind, his face dark and dangerous. She saw Lars stuck underwater trying to talk, but only bubbles came out and he couldn't swim—what was he saying? And then she poured all the booze down the sink and smashed all the bottles, and when she came back to herself, she had stopped shaking and was weak and gutted and somehow brand new.

Chapter Eleven

A FAMILY of deer lived in the deepest recesses of the Nickerson land where it joined the marsh. They were shy and tended to stay hidden, especially around hunting season. That spring a new fawn was born with a taste for danger and rhododendron buds. He had first discovered these tender delicacies on a wild bush deep in his home woods, and they were so good he had polished off every bud there by the following afternoon. He knew he shouldn't leave the safety of home, but he could smell more rhododendron buds just south of where he lived, and he was drawn to eat them as well.

And so he found himself in Old Pete's garden on a morning in early July with a mouth full of flowering pumpkin vines, which tasted even better than the intended rhododendron buds. The fence had proved a small deterrent as he delicately stepped over it, and he was well into the field when Pete caught him red-handed.

Pete saw him from his kitchen window first thing that morning. The fawn was young, and actually looked quite fetching in the early light, but the ruined pumpkin vines were another story altogether. Pete hadn't wasted time thinking, he grabbed a broom and a garden rake and charged full throttle, shouting incoherently, across the lawn and into the garden. The fawn froze. It was his first real encounter with a human being. The noise was unconscionable, and what were those long things it was waving at him? He backed up towards the fence, lept over it, and lept again to avoid the black cat that was closing in on him from behind. Fleeing, he narrowly avoided being hit by a builder's truck as he darted across the street and vanished into the thick woods on the Nickerson land. He had suddenly acquired a new appreciation for the rule about not leaving the woods.

Pete surveyed the devastation. This was a huge setback to his plans for winning the fall pumpkin contest. All of the vines but one were destroyed, and it was too late in the season to plant more seeds. He surveyed the hoof marks and the disturbed soil while Rasputin joined him with a sympathetic air.

"Well Raspy, we're going to need a bigger fence."

The cat mewed. He was pretty sure the fawn wouldn't be back. Glancing toward where the fawn had vanished into the woods, Pete noticed something pink fluttering in the breeze amongst the trees. Crossing the street for a better view, he saw the ribbons on the trees slated for cutting and the posts that marked the way deeper and deeper into the land, and was sick at heart.

NORTH BAY CELEBRATED the fourth of July every year with a big parade, and the whole village turned out on Main Street to either watch or take part. The parade route was lined with flags, and there were elaborate floats depicting Revolutionary War scenes and local oddities, such as the Tree of Liberty, or the Shellfishing club which decorated a flatbed with dunes and marsh grass and clam buckets and rakes, and dressed up in waders and various other clamming gear. There was the dog division, where local dogs donned red, white, and blue and were led in a group, and the fire department joined with their oldest fire trucks, from which they tossed candy. The high school band performed, the oystermen decorated their skiffs, and the kids wore costumes and decorated their bikes. The prize committee awarded a series of ribbons for best costume and decoration. The Fourth of July in North Bay was a slice of old time Americana.

That year the holiday dawned hot and humid, and everyone was anticipating the cool water at the beach after the parade. After a quick coffee, Olive and Johnny started down Main Street to secure a good vantage from which to view the festivities. Olive could remember marching with a group of kids a few summers when she was staying with Eartha, but this was the first parade she'd seen in years. While the world had certainly changed in that time, she was amazed to find the parade the same as ever.

As they walked, Pete drove by in his old woody covered in patriotic bunting, leaning hard on the aroooha horn and making for the parade's start line. Ann rode shotgun, he had invited her to toss candy out to the kids, and she had big bags of it stowed beneath her seat. Olive and Johnny eventually found a bit of stonewall under the shade of a horse chestnut tree, and they cheered and waved with everyone else. When the parade had passed, they followed its wake to stop at the Sea Urchin for a glass of cold lemonade and a brownie, then on into the field at the end of town for the greased pole contest, the three legged race, and the pie eating contest.

Jean was watching the three legged race as the kids competing tripped and got back up to stagger along and the crowd cheered. Douglas Dunn was the last thing on her mind, so she was surprised when he approached her. The last time they had spoken was towards the end of her marriage with Lars when he asked her one final time to give him a chance. He had been asking since high school, since the day she rode off on the back of Lars' bike, and she had been saying no all that time. When he materialized from the crowd she tried to go around him as best she could but he blocked her way and said, "It's too late Jean, Lars is staying in the hospital. Why don't you and me-"

She walked around his other side and he took her arm. "You'll see, you'll finally see, he's gone, Jean, and I'm here. I'm waiting for you, Jean," he said.

She tore away, regretting the crowd and heat. She still felt fragile, but then she saw Olive and knew she had one more thing to do, despite Douglas' latest foul move.

Olive was standing in line for a bottle of water when she noticed Jean. She looked pale and a bit drawn, but she had a small flag tucked into her ponytail, and she was heading her way. Olive took a step back but was hemmed in by a joyfully oblivious crowd.

"You're Olive," Jean stated. She had recognized the red hair from a distance.

Olive regarded Jean carefully.

"I wanted to apologize for what happened the night—"

"The night Lars crashed?"

"Yes. I'm sorry. If I could take it back, I would. I only

want him to wake up. And when he does, I'll wish him well, and I won't bother you again."

Jean stood out pale and ineffably sad in the tanned, happy summer crowd. She was only just home from East House and was working so hard to fix things and keep herself straight. She stood tall and Olive felt her quiet strength.

"Thank you, Jean."

"JEAN WAS a golden girl when they were young," Elea said of her son's ex-wife. She and Olive were sitting with Lars, hoping he'd wake up. Each day, Olive checked in at the hospital, and each day, there was no change. The doctors were patient, but they couldn't completely hide their increasing concern. The longer Lars remained insensible, the more dangerous the situation became. It had been a week already, and talk of transferring to the bigger hospital in Boston had begun.

"They were married right out of school. They couldn't wait, and they were happy for a time. Did you know she was class valedictorian? She'd been accepted at Brown University, not that far away, but she stayed home and got married. I advised her to wait, told her to go to college, but I think she was searching for a foundation. Her home life had been rocky, to say the least, and Lars was, if anything, rock-solid. He was selling real estate hand over fist, and she was running a shop in Hyannis. They were happy to stay in North Bay, and then things started to change. I wondered if she was frustrated. She should have been a CEO in some big company. There were too many late nights, too many bars, too much booze. It hit Lars hard, and as he sank with it, his business did too. After he lost it, he tried to quit drinking three times, and the third time was the charm. But Jean couldn't stop, and it became impossible. There were scenes and fighting, and the golden girl disappeared. They were divorced five years ago, and since then, Lars has devoted himself to protecting the land he used to sell. I've often wondered if it was an atonement of sorts."

It was a lot to digest. And it made a lot of sense. The two women had become friends, and through Elea, Olive was learning Lars' story. He was a great one for practical jokes. He'd once had his mother running through the woods looking for an escaped parrot that wasn't really there. He was an avid sailor and had been quite competitive as a kid, and his first car had been a motorbike.

"They never did have children," Elea said, holding Lars' hand. Both women gazed through the window at the water in the distance, and Olive hoped Lars knew it was there.

JOHNNY AND ANN vowed to make a tradition of it and spend every future Fourth of July in North Bay. They were utterly charmed by the village celebration, and they had spent the remainder of the day at the beach, watching the tide go out and come back in again, walking the flats, and swimming the creeks they found as they explored the marsh. They gave the fireworks a miss and were happy to return home that evening for a late cookout involving a pot of lobsters. It was the kind of meal you don't need to change out of your bathing suit for, and by the end of it, they were pretty much covered in lobster, and mostly in agreement that it had been a welcome change from chowder.

Fun was fun, but first thing on July 5th, Johnny was researching grants, and finding big discrepancies between the dates of application and the date by which they needed the funding. They just didn't have the time.

"This is just another reason land gets cleared," he announced to Olive. She was sitting opposite him at the kitchen table, and they were both peering intently at their laptops.

"We need to luck into something with a rolling application and a quick response," Olive replied.

Insects droned in the warm summer air, and it was hard to stay inside.

Rasputin loped inside with one eye on the pair at the table and one on the old lady, who was floating around the ceiling with her usual agility. She was telling him she thought she might be floating right on out the window to who knows where sometime soon. She had the idea she had to go somewhere for the first time in years.

Olive reached for her cardigan despite the heat and poured another cup of coffee.

In the end, it was Tenny at the historical society who nudged them forward. Johnny had handed him Maisy's journal and the family bible full of Mahitables, and Tenny had handed back a list of likely land preservation foundations.

Chapter Twelve

In the skies above southern Sudan, the wind changed to the southwest and Mikana was sure he felt the exact moment the dry season gave way to the precious, rain-bearing clouds all farmers scan the July sky for. His cattle felt it, too, and began to stir, lowing with more energy than they'd had in days. The skies darkened with fat clouds, and heavy drops began to fall. In the villages and towns around Khartoum, the children ran out to play in the rain, and in the city, people sat under covered terraces and watched it pour. They were all released from the relentless heat, and the fields and the animals were watered, and another year's crops secured. The rain rode along a low-pressure trough accompanied by thunder and lightning and then moved across the African continent toward the Atlantic ocean.

ANN THOUGHT she had never been so hot. It was humid and sticky and the only place to be was in the cool ocean. Short of that, she was looking for air conditioning, but that was spotty on Cape Cod. As the screen door of the Sea Urchin thumped shut behind her, she resigned herself to the heat but hoped for the sake of the staff that the kitchen was air-conditioned. She sat down at the bar and asked for a cup of chowder.

By now she had tasted chowder up and down the Cape, and each one was different. She was beginning to think of chowder as a genre more than a specifically defined dish; each one was unique to its cook and possibly unique to the variable conditions under which it was created. It couldn't be pinned down easily, but herbs were involved, and infinite patience. Luckily she still had a few more weeks to nail it.

The Sea Urchin was quiet in the heat. It was more of a beach day than an out for lunch day, and Macy Jones, who had owned the restaurant for 30 years, set the cup down in front of Ann with a friendly smile and a packet of oyster crackers. Ann ignored the crackers as she always did and picked up the spoon.

One taste and she knew.

"Who makes the chowder?" she asked.

"I do," Macy said.

It was perfectly balanced. The broth was neither thick nor thin and it was salted just right.

"It's the salt, that's it! How did you get the salt to balance the flavor like that?"

Not many people could narrow down the taste of her chowder to that extent. Macy was impressed.

"You want the secret?" she asked.

Ann nodded and took another bite.

Macy couldn't divulge her whole recipe, and it wouldn't matter if she had, because chowder truly was stamped by the cook, the ingredients at hand, and the humor of the moment, but she was always happy to share the secret behind the chowder. Food was meant to be shared generously, and no one in North Bay was more generous than Macy Jones, who had employed several generations of locals as she catered their weddings and funerals and served their dinners and drinks from the Sea Urchin.

"No salt," she said.

Ann let the flavor play across her palate.

"Count on the salt pork or bacon to add salt. Let the clams or the quahogs add their salt. Never add a grain of it to your chowder. That's how the balance happens. It's so simple most people overlook it. Of course, you could take this whole conversation with a grain of salt," Macy grinned, "but I wouldn't."

Ann scraped the cup clean. She needed a basket of littlenecks.

"When's low tide?"

Macy looked out at the marsh. "About three hours."

She couldn't wait to go clamming. The final recipe was forming in her mind. Fewer herbs and no salt to bring out the simple essence of the chowder itself. The heat and the humidity were forgotten.

"Thank you, Macy"

MIA'S DESK at Save the Land was piled high with applications for land preservation grants. It was important to her that the foundation offered awards on a rolling basis because sometimes when land was threatened by imminent destruction, there simply wasn't time to wait for the next application period or the new round of funding. She looked outside. Her own California countryside outside her office window continued to be browner by the day, and she was trying not to be too concerned about the fire warnings that were daily becoming more urgent as the season got hotter and hotter.

"Here's one in a great location," Jane, her partner in all things preservation, held up an application.

"Look at this, 15-acres, untouched, on Cape Cod and they want to clear cut it." She handed over the printout.

Mia ran the map and lot numbers and couldn't believe the match.

"The Nickerson land. They have two weeks to fund a buyout for the developer. Jane, I'm heading to the Cape." Away from this dry heat. She could already feel the pull of the cool Atlantic and the land she had never seen—and she had a large sum of proceeds from that very land burning a hole in her pocket.

"Can you work out how much we can award them towards saving it? I know about that place, it's been untouched for centuries. That kind of land is why we exist as a foundation. I'm going out there to see it myself, and I need a figure." She was already planning to add her proceeds to whatever the foundation could offer.

THAT MORNING DOUGLAS DUNN arrived at the Nickerson land a bit before the bulldozers. He was certain his plans would ultimately receive approval from the Preservation Society and keen to set things in motion. He wanted to make sure the bulldozers reached the site and got situated without any problems. He didn't expect interference, but who knew? He walked the path already marked by posts and ribbons hanging limp in the heat and regarded the trees above. He smelled salt and pine sap, and heard droning insects, and for a moment the trees seemed to be bearing down on him, and he remembered his quiet, reticent father who had died when a saw snapped cutting a tree, and hating trees all over again, he walked back up to the street where two bulldozers where arriving on the beds of large trucks, and showed them where to park. He made sure to position the bulldozers facing the trees, and he didn't see the observant fawn run silently through the heat to tell his grandfather the stag of the huge, yellow beasts.

At Silver Beech, they spent the warm, humid evening on the screened-in side of the porch eating the latest incarnation of clam chowder and listening to slow, smooth blues on the old gramophone. Pete was there too, contributing dried herbs this time thinking that fresh ones were too intense. The candle on the table burned straight and dripless, and there was no sign of a breeze.

"There's a house down the street, has a stream running under it," Pete said.

"Under it?" Johnny asked.

"Yep, under it," Pete nodded. "And one day, sometime in the 1800s, it was really hot, like it is today, and the stream was cool, and a little girl who was trying to cool down or chasing a ball, or some such, drowned in the stream. They say she's still there."

The air on the porch was still.

"I've heard about that house. Tenny at historic says

people have seen a naked lady dancing in an upstairs window. That's a good one. Hey Ann, I think this is the chowder. I mean it, you've hit it. And no sherry. What's the secret ingredient?"

"There's not a secret ingredient. But rather a secret non-ingredient: no salt. I heard it today at the Sea Urchin from a non-ghost. This is it. I'm entering it in this fall's *Boston's Best* chowder contest."

"No salt, huh?" Johnny was impressed. "Damn it's hot. Pete, let's have that salad."

Pete had picked all of his lettuce that afternoon before it could bolt in the heat, so they had a huge bowl of beautiful green leaves dressed in the lightest of vinaigrettes. Ann had rigged up a series of fans across the kitchen to make cooking viable, and as soon as she had completed the chowder she'd run down to the ocean and plunged in.

"Sure seems hotter than ever," Pete said.

They were all feeling the heat. Even Johnny was a bit lackluster with the humidity that evening.

"Used to get hot maybe a week or two in August, and we'd all go sleep on the porch, but the weatherman says this one's going to last at least a week or more, and it's only middle of July. Don't like to bring it up, but if they clear the Nickerson land, sure is going to feel hotter around the place, isn't it?" Pete said with a glance toward the woods. "Those trees cool the air, they do." Everyone thought of the bull-dozers sitting just yards away, and the ribbons in the trees, and the stakes. The threat was as palpable as the heat.

"Olive, did you see the grant for Save the Land? Tenny dug it up. It has a revolving application schedule," Johnny said.

"Already done." She looked at the chowder pot, it was

still half full.

Following her gaze, Ann said, "You know what? I think if we let this sit, the flavors might develop even more by tomorrow. What if chowder should be served a day after you make it?" She picked up the pot and headed toward the kitchen to put it away from the heat.

Johnny played the steamiest record he had: Summertime from Porgy and Bess.

"Abby Mitchell, 1935," Pete said.

"Marvelous! How did you know?" Johnny asked.

"I was there. Or rather here—Eartha's mother played it here when we were kids. Years ago. Takes me back."

"I pulled it out of the barn the other day. Do you see how heavy that record is? You can warm those things up in the oven and reshape them, make them into ashtrays." Johnny said.

"Sure can," Pete said.

Rasputin was stretched out against the screen side of the porch, looking twice his length and trying to catch a breeze, the way hot cats do. The old lady sailed through the candle flame and smiled at him as she went by.

The candle flickered, and Olive shivered despite the heat.

"What *is* it about this place?" she asked.

Everyone looked around as the last chords of Summertime faded. It was a little creepy: sitting in the candle-lit porch with the sheer presence of the Nickerson land palpable just beyond the screen. "Maybe it's the woods. They're older than anything else here," Johnny said, thinking them even more precious for facing the bulldozers.

"Oh, it's the woods, and it's the house too—this house, and my house, and most of them. Eartha's mother was a very logical study, but one time we were sitting in the dining room and she looked up and said, 'That was a ghost.' Just like that. And she's the last person I'd think would go around seeing ghosts. House in Cotuit even had to call in an exorcist once, I hear," Pete said.

"They did? No!" said Johnny, breaking the spell so they could all laugh.

"Think they needed chowder?" Ann hooted.

"Eddie Cochran, 1958," Johnny placed Summertime Blues on the turntable and cranked it up. "The barn's full of great music. I keep finding this stuff. I think we should do a music exhibit at the museum. That would generate a lot of attention, it's a great way to make history fun. We could round up old radios, and record players and gramophones and have a proper rave of it. Maybe make it a monster mash —invite the ghosts as well! Too bad it's too hot to dance now," he said.

"I can bring some of the leftover chowder to Lars' parents," Olive said, a bit more seriously. The wait for Lars continued, and the new word at the hospital was *coma*. There was a lot the doctors didn't know about head injuries, although they said his eyes seemed to be responding to light in a way they hadn't before, which was a positive development. They thought it was best not to move him, so he'd stay on Cape Cod, and his parents and Olive, by extension, stayed hopeful. She'd just been there that afternoon, and the air conditioning had been a blessing after a hot morning applying for land grants. His room was full of flowers and cards, and she was touched by how the community had reached out. She sat with him for an hour each day and it felt familiar, and she was sure that if he'd just wake up, she could figure out why.

Chapter Thirteen

Thousands of miles to the east, another cape, Ponta Delgada in the Azores, basked under clear skies and summer sun. Tourists thronged the beaches; the water was cool, the seafood delicious, and the local wines refreshing. It was perfect weather to explore the eclectic architecture of the city and the beautiful gardens of the countryside surrounding it. Not many people thought back to a time when the Azores were the last point of land where a ship could stock up for the long trip across the Atlantic to the Americas, perhaps even Cape Cod. Everyone was too busy enjoying themselves to notice the low-pressure trough from Sudan caught up by the strong high-pressure system over the Azores hurling west toward the Caribbean on a track not too different from that followed by the sailing ships of yesteryear. Soon after, weather buoys in the North Atlantic reported a tropical disturbance heading straight for Bermuda, complete with thunder, rain, and intensifying winds.

LARS FOLLOWED the landscape with a bird's eye view. He could see the marsh where the land met the sea, and he could see how the water was encroaching further and further inland. He saw a line of trees killed by the encroaching salt-water where a dairy pasture had been in his youth, and if the ocean breached the ridge behind the trees, the field would flood for good. His view was not only of this time, but of all time, and he could see back to the grazing cows, and far beyond even to a time when there was only ice. And forward again in time, and the pristine green narrow strip of land gleamed untouched in the blue ocean. Then the first people came, and he saw they had managed the forest as a game park, taking only what they needed, and in places, it looked a lot like the Nickerson land did now, only on today's Nickerson land the brush had closed in along the tree trunks where the first people had cleared it and kept it open to encourage game. Then he moved through time again and saw how the landscape was in constant motion as the ocean took a bit of land here and gave back a bit there, while the marsh and dunes protected the higher ground from storms and big tides. And he could see how that balance could be so quickly overwhelmed as the tides and the storms increased in strength, and the land was put to profit and not to preservation, and then he winced and closed his eyes against a bright light, and saw green eyes and red hair, and heard his mother telling him years ago he must never stare directly at the sun.

Chapter Fourteen

Bob Marcus watched the sky turn from blue to gray from the deck of his 30-foot marlin boat just off the Bermuda coast. It was so early in the season and they'd been hauling in so many fish, he hadn't given much thought to the forecast. The day had started sunny, as the air changed he was sure he could smell a low-pressure front coming in from the east. He'd spent most of his life at sea, and his nose was pretty accurate, so he tuned in to his CB radio reluctantly because as soon as he confirmed his suspicion, they'd have to go into harbor. Sure enough, they were sitting in the path of an intensifying low-pressure area that was looking to organize into a coherent weather system. "Ian! Weather coming in! Turn her about and head in!" he shouted to his brother at the helm. Ian corrected their course and Bob started hauling in lines. A collective groan issued from his sportfishing passengers as the boat came around and pointed toward land. "Better safe than sorry," he told them.

THE HEAT WAS RELENTLESS, with gunmetal gray skies and humidity close to a hundred percent. A sulfurous stink rose from the marsh at low tide, and nature waited for rain while lawns turned brown and gardens wilted. It takes three days of heat over 90 degrees to make a heatwave. This was day four, and it was still only mid-July.

Old Pete had heard the state recommendation that everyone hold off watering to preserve precious supplies. He was quite happy to let his lawn wither, but certainly not his garden, so he watered sparingly in the cool of the very early morning. At his age, he was up early anyway. Today, Rasputin loped across the street to join him and play in the cool water. Pete didn't know many water cats, but Raspy sure liked to cool his jets just next to the sprinkler, or the hose, or whatever source of water he could find. Especially in a heatwave. They both avoided looking at the bulldozers.

The pumpkin vine was taking over the far end of the garden, and it was covered with big, beautiful, orange blossoms. In retrospect, the deer attack might well have been a boon, as it had cleared out the competing vines and left plenty of space for the one survivor to flourish. Pete wondered why in all these years he hadn't thought of that himself. Less really can be more, he supposed, wondering if each blossom would go all out pumpkin. As he surveyed his garden, Pete realized the morning was quiet. There was no birdsong and no rustle of the leaves in the trees, no turkeys calling, none of the usual din put forth by nature. And the air pressure was so low it could give you a headache. He'd seen plenty of bad storms in his time, and this is how it felt just before one hit. He shook his head. A hurricane this early? It was so hot, he finally just held the sprinkler over his head while Rasputin danced around at his heels in the dripping water. They both felt better for it.

OLIVE FLIPPED ON the radio in the kitchen as she filled the coffee pot. She started every morning with NPR while she puttered around, only today it was too hot to putter, and she was wondering if she should break with tradition and try an iced coffee instead of her usual hot brew.

"The season's first named storm has formed overnight off the coast of Bermuda. The National Hurricane Center states subtropical storm Argo is located 150 miles southwest of Bermuda and heading north on a course just offshore of the island with maximum sustained winds at 50 miles per hour. Forecasters are watching closely to track the storm's path. Early models point to possible landfall in southeastern New England with increased winds and no sign yet of dissipation."

"A hurricane!" Johnny grabbed a cup and filled it. "It's too early for a hurricane, but it sure would break the heat."

"Please continue to monitor the forecast over the next few days as we track this possibly fast-moving and threatening coastal storm system." The NPR forecast shifted to the Boston news, where broadcasters were also remarking on the heat and how early in the season it was for a hurricane.

"Argo! Must be one of the Argonauts," Johnny mused.

DOUGLAS DUNN HATED WAITING. The final survey of the Nickerson land before clearing was scheduled for early the next morning, but the crew was balking as the hurricane forecast firmed up. No way they were coming down to the

Cape to get stuck in a major storm. Plans would have to wait until the storm changed track or passed over, and he was going to have to wait with it. There was nothing he could do but tell his bosses at Moraine and bide the time in his big air conditioned house. The heat was rising with the humidity, and Don had reported Lars remained unconscious. He lit a cigarette, tuned on the storm report and watched the ocean for signs of the weather.

MIA FLEW into Boston's Logan Airport at 2:00 that afternoon. The humidity and the heat hit hard as she disembarked from the plane and set out from the terminal in a rented car toward North Bay. The navigation on her dashboard showed a mostly straight shot out of the city and south onto Route 3 to the Sagamore Bridge over the Cape Cod Canal. She was well on her way by 3:30, so she missed the rush hour traffic, and as she drove, she wondered what she was going to do once she arrived. She was pretty sure she was the first member of the Nickerson family to see the land since at least 1935, and she and Jane had worked out that if Save the Land slightly exceeded her proceeds from her brother's original sale of it they would have enough to buy it back from the developer. Mia was certain of only two things: she wouldn't inform her brother until after the fact, and before she actually did save the land, she wanted to see it.

She recognized the iconic arch of the Sagamore Bridge in the distance from pictures she had seen, and as she crossed it, she relished the view of the ocean and land from its highest point before descending to the Mid-Cape Highway. She could smell the salt of the ocean and the deeper brine of the marsh. The air was gray and soupy, in complete contrast to the dry heat of California.

She found her host friendly and talkative as she checked into her B&B in the center of North Bay. The house was charming and an easy walking distance from most things, including the beach and the village shops and watering holes.

"Might be a hurricane coming," her host said and handed her the keys.

Mia sighed. Fires on the West Coast and hurricanes on the East Coast. Two elements: fire and water. Add some wind, and well, she wouldn't think about it at the moment. After a cold shower, she used her phone to map her way and started walking toward the Nickerson land.

It was slow going in the heat, but her unhurried pace allowed her to take in just how old things were in North Bay. Her route along the historic highway was lined with ancient gray stone walls and towering trees set before antique houses. Some of them were classic Capes with central chimneys and low rooflines dating from before the Revolutionary War, and some were more recent, Queen Anne or even Georgian. Mia noticed the front porches and lawns, and everything looked brown and tired due to the heat.

She walked on until her phone announced that she had arrived at her destination. She saw nothing but a thick grove of trees behind a stone wall: magnificent old trees, and underbrush, and what looked like a path into it. Then she saw the pink ribbons marking the doomed trees, and the posts driven into the ground, and the two bulldozers facing the trees. She shivered despite the heat and looked around. The silence was uncanny. She didn't see anyone, so she plunged right into the woods and made for the path.

The land rose slightly at first. There were oak trees and pine trees, and huge stately maples. There were raspberry canes, rhododendrons, and wild blueberry bushes. She smelled pine sap and salt. She passed huge glacial rocks, remembering to avoid the rampant poison ivy while the mosquitoes pestered her like B-52 bombers.

Then the land began a gentle descent, and the mosquitoes got worse. The woods gradually gave way, first to grasses then finally to rocks, until Mia found herself in the marsh. The gray-green marsh grass stretched before her to meet the horizon where the gray of the ocean met the gray of the sky, and she couldn't tell which was which.

This was the Nickerson land her brother had sold to developers. The ribbons went right to the marsh.

This was the land in the old family story her grandfather had told. One brother had died here and one had not.

She followed the line of the marsh. The solid land gave way quickly to mud and marsh grass, and she could see the creeks leading out to deeper water. They were empty and she used her phone to confirm it was low tide. She imagined cranberries here in fall, and ducks, and fat fish in the creeks at high tide. The aroma was rank and raw, and it stank in the heat. When she came to a stone wall heading back in the direction she had come, she followed it through thick trees and vegetation. She thought it must be an old field boundary. In contrast to the wildness on her side of the wall, the land opposite was lawn heading down to the marsh, with Adirondack chairs arranged to take in the view of the marsh, the ocean, and the sunset.

She could only imagine what lived here: fish and fowl and insects. An ecosystem supported by the trees and the grasses. Crickets and tree frogs. Deer and coyotes. Foxes and raccoons. The marsh itself was precious as a briney habitat and as a barrier between the land and the rising ocean. She noticed the wide girth of the trees, which indicated their advanced age, giving evidence that this land had indeed been untouched for a very long time. She came upon a kettle hole, a swampy low-lying place that dated back to the glaciers and provided fresh water to the animals here. Now the mosquitos attacked in earnest, and she hurried her pace to make higher ground. A rooftop came into view among the trees.

The stone wall went straight and true back to the road she had started from, only now she was on the far side of the Nickerson land. Across the street, she saw another stone wall and a low-roofed Cape house with white clapboards, yellow trim, and a massive central chimney. Next to it was a huge garden. To her right, she saw a magnificent silver beech tree, and behind it, a house with a big front porch. An old, brown delivery van stood in front of a much older barn. A few cars passed on the road, but otherwise, everything was quiet in the early evening heat. She was sure she was looking at the house her grandfather had sold in 1935. Just as she was wondering why they had never come to see this extraordinary place, a black cat came mewing and wound itself between her legs.

Chapter Fifteen

In the Carolinas, Megan Clark was driving a station wagon with two kids and a dog in the backseat. They were leaving the outer beach and heading to her parents' place on higher ground. She had filled the car with gas and water bottles and stowed food in coolers of ice, and was fairly certain they'd left in time to get there safely. She called her mother on her cell phone and told her not to worry. Tropical storm Argo had just brushed the Bahamas, causing flooding and some structural damage but no loss of life. Its winds were intensifying to hurricane strength as it moved over the open ocean and turned north for the Carolinas.

A⏏ ᴅᴀᴡɴ ᴛʜᴇ ɴᴇxᴛ ᴍᴏʀɴɪɴɢ, the wind stirred just enough to move the curtain in old Pete's window. It was just enough to wake him, and as it did, he felt the weather shift and knew something was coming. Olive made coffee while listening to the news that tropical storm Argo had blown up to hurricane strength with winds of 110 miles per hour when it hit the outer banks of the Carolinas, turned back out the sea to feed on the warm water, and then turned slightly north-northeast with increasing wind strength. The local news was warning of landfall just off Cape in Plymouth the following evening and telling everyone it was time to pull boats out of the water and hunker down.

Cape Cod is only 15 miles across at its widest point, and the long arm of it sticks 75 miles out into the Atlantic Ocean. People there have a long history of storms, some of which are named and some of which are not, some deadly and some not, and the worst of the storms live on in local memory and legend. If the forecasters were right, this might be one of the big ones, and someday people would ask each other where they had been when Hurricane Argo struck.

Jᴏʜɴɴʏ ʜᴀᴅ ɴᴇᴠᴇʀ ʙᴇᴇɴ on Cape Cod during a hurricane. In the village, he saw people stocking up on supplies: bottled water, food, ice, and anything else they thought they might need. It was busy and hectic, and he had to wait in line at a gas station to fill his tank with about a hundred other people doing the same thing. At the harbor, he found the square red and black hurricane flags starting to stir in a slowly building breeze that did little to dispel the heat. The boat ramp was mobbed with people and trucks hauling trailers back and forth, pulling boats and dumping them on the parking lot before turning around and going back for more. He parked the brown van well out of the way, walked down to help, and found himself on a launch going out to bring in the bigger boats from outside the harbor. The marina guys shouted out instructions and he was soon soaking wet and, as much as he hated to admit it, completely caught up in the excitement of the moment. A hurricane is many things. Exciting is one of them, and he could almost feel the wind and the water preparing to put aside their usual calm raiment for much more wild attire.

ANN AND OLIVE were moving everything that wasn't nailed down into the barn. If the wind got strong enough it could pick up loose objects and send them right through the windows. As they removed the wicker furniture from the porch, they began to appreciate the sheer volume of things not only in but also around the house. Next, they'd go help Pete, and then someone had to get in food and ice. Ann could remember storms in Marblehead that had stopped everything—food trucks, ice trucks, and the mail—for an entire week.

RASPUTIN WAS SITTING on Olive's phone when it rang. In all the confusion, she was lucky to hear it, and besides, she was waiting to hear from her parents and maybe Lars' mother.

"Olive Adams? My name is Mia Nickerson. I'm with Save the Land. I received your application for a preservation grant last week."

Olive turned in her tracks to enter the library for some quiet and sat down.

"Can we meet?"

"You're here?" Olive asked.

"I flew into Boston yesterday, I guess just ahead of the storm of the century," Mia said, half in jest.

Olive felt hope soaring and told herself to calm down.

"Yes, of course. How about later today? I need to batten down the hatches. We should have time late this afternoon before anything hits, I think. Can you come here to Silver Beech?" It made sense. It was about the Nickerson land and the Nickerson land was here.

"5:00 alright?"

"Yes, plan on an early supper with us," Olive said, unsure how she'd pull that together under the current circumstances.

She put the phone down and whooped with excitement.

THE HOSPITAL WAS one of the only places guaranteed to maintain power through any kind of weather. It had not one, but two electrical feeds from different substations, and in preparation for big storms, the diesel tanks that fueled the generators on the roof were always filled to capacity. Hospital staff did everything they could to keep things running as normal, and some even stayed overnight as long as they were needed when conditions outside really deteriorated.

"I'm staying through the storm with Lars," Elea told Olive that afternoon when she stopped in for a quick visit.

Olive wasn't usually a great fan of hospitals, but today

this one seemed like an oasis of calm in the face of the coming storm.

"Kurt can manage the house, I'll be here, so don't worry about it," Elea knew Olive had her own house to manage.

As tempted as she was to share the news about Save the Land, Olive held off. She didn't want to build false hope, and there was enough going on already. She had also opted not to mention the surveyors posts, the pink ribbons, and the bulldozers. She didn't want to build a sense of hopelessness either.

"There it is again!" Elea called out with a huge smile. "I'm certain he's trying to squeeze my hand. It's the second time I've felt it. The doctors aren't convinced, but I've also seen his eyes moving around a bit and I'm sure he's trying to come back."

ANN TOOK one look around Maki's, the village store, noted the emptying shelves, and drove straight on into Hyannis. The larger town would hopefully have something left on supermarket shelves. She found a jammed parking lot, which didn't bode well, and inside the store the aisles were hectic. She got ice first, and some fresh food for tonight and tomorrow. Next she hit the canned food aisle—baked beans and tuna— then on to the dried goods: pasta, rice, more pasta, some jars of sauce. Better get enough for Pete, too. His kitchen hadn't seemed too full as they moved in his outdoor things earlier that day. She stood in the crowded aisle for a moment and contemplated how to make canned food delicious before grabbing paper plates and plastic spoons against the probable lack of hot water to wash proper dishes once the power went out. Then she remembered coffee. She got the last can of Maxwell House and sighed with relief. Once after a storm on the north shore she had gone a week without a cup, and that had been a very long week indeed. Cat food! Need to feed Rasputin, and surprisingly, she didn't even think about cigarettes as she finally stood in the long line at the checkout counter.

Coming back through the village, Johnny saw windows being covered with sheets of plywood to protect the glass from windblown objects. He was soaking wet and hot in the oppressive humidity as the van radio prophesied doom from wild winds and an accompanying storm surge of water to boot. Argo was currently a category two storm out at sea on a course headed straight for them. The hope was that it would veer out to sea at the last minute, or the wind would reduce to something a bit more manageable if it did hit land.

He had made friends with at least half the village as he pulled boats, and by now, the harbor was pretty much empty. Macy from the Sea Urchin had come down earlier with a huge pot of chowder for them. It was what she had left after giving the rest away to her staff. There was no way she'd be able to keep it fresh when the power went out, so she had heated it up and brought it down for the boat pullers.

"Remember the year the wrack line went all the way up beyond the street and left a line of ruined boats behind it?" She had asked as she handed out paper cups full of chowder.

"Won't be happening this time, we got them all out," boasted Sean, Johnny's new friend from the launch.

"And in 1998, we had one where all the clams washed up into the street, and I steamed them over my grill and had a fine supper. Easiest clamming ever, just picked them up," she said.

Soon they were all slurping chowder and remembering other storms.

"How about the one that put a tree through the brand new roof on the historical society?"

"Or the one that took a porch off one house and attached it to another?"

"And the Halloween storm that took the boathouse from the harbor and it floated away and we never found it?"

Johnny was fascinated by the stories and feeling how the weather played such a defining role in life here. He thought about that other storm long ago in Maisy Hale's journal.

"Johnny, come have a beer with us at the Urchin before this gets too out of hand," his new friend Sean said.

THE BREEZE WAS BECOMING a wind as the day passed, and it seemed to make people move with all the more urgency. Olive made sure her parents were fine down in Truro, and then found Pete with Rasputin in his garden.

"Will you look at that pumpkin vine!" he said.

It was growing bigger each day.

"Sure could use the rain, but I'm a bit worried about the wind," he looked at the trees and wondered which might break and fall onto his garden.

"Not much to be done about it now, I guess."

Earlier that day, they had made sure his house was as ready as it would ever be for the coming storm.

"Pete, will you bring Rasputin home at about five this afternoon, and then plan on supper with us?"

"Sure will. I'll bring vegetables. Lots of vegetables," he said.

MACY CLOSED down the Sea Urchin just before 4:30. She wanted her staff to have time to get home before the storm hit, and she knew they probably still had to prepare for it.

Bit by bit, North Bay grew quieter as people headed home before the storm. Johnny exchanged phone numbers with a couple of new friends and, inspired by the beer, headed over to Maki's store at the last minute. He found the last two bottles of dry white on the shelf along with a few loaves of bread and some ice cream. He was the last customer there and the shelves were empty. The street was empty too. As he drove back to Silver Beech, he noticed the wind rising and seeming to talk through the trees, and the light fading, even though evening was still far off, and the humidity stifling all of it. He sat, wet and salty, in the van, and decided not to park anywhere near the silver beech tree in front of the house. He opted instead for the open field on the far side of the Nickerson land where he saw Olive and Ann's cars parked already. The porch was bare of furniture, the barn was shut tight, and the house looked a bit forlorn as he thumped open the screen door to the kitchen and heard the radio.

'Hurricane Argo is expected to make landfall late tonight in Rhode Island. If you have any preparations to make, make them now. This is a life-threatening storm. Hurricane Argo is moving north- northeast toward Rhode Island, and surface winds are measuring at 125 miles an hour as the storm heads north. Local hurricane shelters are open across the Cape and Islands. Find the closest to you on Cape and Island storm shelter dot com. The governor has issued a statement urging all residents to refrain from nonessential travel beginning at 9:00 tonight to allow emergency vehicles to move as effectively as possible. This is National Public Radio Boston. Now back to our regular programming.'

Chapter Sixteen

THE FIRST RAINDROPS fell at around five o'clock that afternoon. Ann heard them patter onto the window over the kitchen sink as she peeled potatoes for another round of chowder. She had stopped at the fish market last thing on her way past the village, just in case something good was going. She scored a pint of shelled clams on the cheap in anticipation that the power wouldn't hold up long against the projected winds. She was one batch away from committing the recipe to paper, and it was the perfect project for a few days with no electricity. Her pencils were sharp and her notebooks were ready.

"Chowder again? Marvelous," said a recently showered and refreshed Johnny.

"And stuffed clams, and Pete's about to get here with vegetables."

They could just hear the wind, and the screen door rattled a bit in its frame. Ann turned on all the lights while Johnny looked for some music to fend off the gathering storm outside.

"You going out in this? Nobody goes out in this." Mia's host at the B & B was incredulous.

"Just across the village, and not for too long. Not to worry."

"Just make sure you stay away from the trees out there, they're likely to start falling if the forecast has it right."

Mia supposed she could have postponed the meeting, but she knew from Olive's grant application that the next (and probably last) meeting with the Historic Preservation Society was just over a week away. Her colleague Jane at Save the Land had confirmed the foundation could exceed her half of the proceeds from the original sale plus kick in a little more to placate the developer. She was anxious to settle the deal as soon as possible. Mia realized she was compelled to go for another reason as well: the land and the house seemed to be calling her.

Her drive across the village was eerie. The light was a dirty gray-brown, and when she glimpsed it, the ocean looked like a dark beast beginning to stir. The trees were moving and the rising wind felt alive. For a moment, she questioned the wisdom of being out on such a night, then checked herself as she added her rental car to the collection of vehicles out in the field past the house.

"Stay away from the trees," her host had said.

CATS ARE the best at making themselves comfortable when weather conditions deteriorate, and Rasputin was no exception. He and Pete had come in the back door, wet from the rain, with a sharp breath of wind behind them. As Pete plunked a big basket of vegetables onto one end of the

kitchen table, Rasputin settled into a cushioned chair at the
other end.

"Picked most of the veggies this afternoon late when the
forecast seemed sure. One year I didn't, and a storm brought
in so much salt from the ocean everything green on land was
dead in two weeks. Salt killed the leaves off the trees, we had
fall with no color in the middle of summer, and it ruined my
garden, too. Best eat it now," he said.

Ann marveled at the wealth of fresh ingredients and
gathered them up. Johnny was setting a special storm table,
and they all felt the anticipation of something coming.

THE EMPTY PORCH felt familiar to Mia, even though she
could think of no reason why it should. The front door had a
deserted air to it, so she continued around to the back, where
she saw lights and heard music.

Olive greeted her warmly and ushered her in, closing the
kitchen door against the rain as she made the introductions:
"Mia, meet Johnny, and Pete, and that's Ann. Please, sit
down." Johnny handed her a glass of wine, and she smelled
the chowder in the pot and took in the old-fashioned kitchen
as the black cat came to wind itself around her legs.

Rasputin glanced up at the ceiling where the old lady
seemed to be dancing. "Not long now, feel the wind?" she
told him in his head.

JEAN HATED STORMS. Always had. Something in the wind
frightened her, the way it seemed to be alive and the way it
seemed to be trying to say something. She was safe at home
and fully prepared for the storm: candles, canned food, some

bottles of water, and no booze to speak of in the house. But as the wind rose, she found it all too hard and decided to go to bed and sleep through the whole thing.

Sleep came and her dreams were as wild as the wind outside.

She was making her valedictorian speech at her high school graduation and the podium blew away and then the stage turned to water. Her graduation robes became fins, and she swam through cresting waves and white caps, and all manner of things were stirred up on the floor of the sea: shipwrecks and chests of gold and drowned sailors. Coming up to the surface, she saw the trees on land bending in the gale, almost obscured by the sheets of rain, and Douglas Dunn was riding the howling wind and throwing lightning from the sky. And she was all the ages she had been and all the people she had been, and she dove again and found Lars still trapped under the ocean, and part of her remembered she'd seen him there before, and he was desperately trying to say something, but his speech came out in bubbles of silent air.

'Hurricane Argo continues on its path toward Rhode Island with a wind speed of 115 miles an hour. Current models project the storm will hit land several hours earlier than previously thought as wind speeds intensify over warm ocean waters. Heavy rains are predicted and worst-case scenarios show the peak of the storm coinciding with high tide. Coastal flooding, rain, and extreme wind warnings are in place. The Massachusetts governor's office requests that you shelter in place. This is a life-threatening storm. Stay tuned to National Public Radio Boston and stay safe.'

"Should have stuck with records," Johnny said. He turned off the radio and flipped on a gentle blues tune.

"Let's check the forecast every half hour or so? Nothing we can do about it anyway. Everyone can bunk down here for the night. You guys ever been to a hurricane party? I think we're kind of having one," Olive said.

The wind was louder, and they had all just sprinted through the big house securing the windows. Most of the windows were old and tended to swell in the heat, which meant they usually stayed open from about June to late September. They'd had quite a struggle closing some, and a few were still cracked open. Johnny hoped the rain didn't find its way through, and Olive was amazed they hadn't thought about it earlier.

Closing the windows was how Mia got to see the house. She had traipsed through every room and felt at home. The place seemed suspended in time, but maybe that was just the antiques, or the storm closing in. Sometimes you just know a place, she supposed. She was generally confident in a situation, but here, in a new house with new people, she was confident and comfortable. She tried to recall her exact connection to this place; her grandfather's grandfather had been born here and lived here before going to California. If her family had somehow visited in her childhood, she doubted her brother would ever have sold the Nickerson land; she knew from her work that dissociation from the land was a major contributing factor to abuse of the land.

THE TREES on the Nickerson land remembered winds like these, especially the older ones, and were prepared to dance with the wind rather than break in it. The animals knew where to hide, and the deer family secreted itself away from the rising water of the creek in the shelter of a huge glacial stone. Every creature, from big to small, had hidden away to wait out the storm. The wind drove the water into the creek and it overflowed. The wind drove sheets of rain before it and struck the house with increasing force, and everyone waited.

"Woody Herman, *Blowing Up a Storm*, 1945. Perfect, right? I found it in the barn this morning while I was hauling out the kerosene lamps," Johnny put the record on, and they sat down to chowder and heaps of fresh vegetables.

The electric lights flickered and the wind sounded just beneath the music.

"Hear that? It's the trees on the Nickerson land moaning," Pete said.

The silver beech out front was having its say, too. They could hear its branches rubbing against each other. Mia chose her moment.

"The Nickerson land. That's what this is about. Olive, I can help you with a grant. I've never seen a piece of land more worthy of saving." She weighed how much to tell. She and Olive were both connected to this house, and it felt right.

Olive had never missed Lars so much. This should have been his moment, too. She found herself speechless with relief.

"Oh, marvelous! Marvelous! More wine!" Johnny filled their glasses. "A toast! To the Nickerson land, long may it flourish; to Save the Land, long may it persevere; and to Mia, who washed ashore in a storm!" Their cheering and clinking glasses temporarily drowned out the sound of the gathering wind, but as they finally sipped the sound came back more wild than ever.

"There's ghosts out there walking tonight," Old Pete put his glass down.

"Speaking of ghosts." Mia looked into the faces gathered around the table and forged ahead: "I have a story to tell you."

The chowder was finished, the wind grew louder, and even the kerosene lamps flickered.

"A story about two brothers fighting over a piece of land and how to use it. One was Thomas Hale, and his brother was crushed by a falling tree in a storm."

The wind howled and the trees protested.

"His brother died on the Nickerson land. Both brothers had grown up in this house. Maybe Thomas was driven by guilt, but he hid his real name and never came back to Cape Cod. People here assumed he was dead, and his mother left the house to her cousin, a Nickerson—"

"Maisy Hale!" Johnny shouted out.

"Yes, my middle name is Maisy!" Mia said. "The Hales and Nickersons were cousins from New England, but they met again in California and through marriage reconnected the families, so my grandfathers going back are both Hale and Nickerson. Thomas explained it all on his deathbed. And he also mentioned the Nickerson land."

"Mia *Maisy* Nickerson!" Johnny said.

"Yes, exactly. So through the marriage of cousins, Thomas's childhood home came back to him, and his last wish was the Nickerson land adjoining the house be preserved. It was all he could do in the memory of his mother and his brother. And so we did preserve it for many years. In 1935, my great-granddad sold this house to a family named Fullerton."

"That's me. My aunt was Eartha Fullerton, she left me the house in April," Olive said.

The two women looked at each other over the table. These were deep connections. The wind was wild outside, pelting the windows with leaves and rain.

"He sold the house, but he kept the Nickerson land back in a trust so it would always be safe. In due time my grandfather left the trust to me and my brother with the proviso that my brother keep the controlling interest. And that's how the land was recently sold to developers."

Mia took a deep breath. It was all out on the table.

The lights flickered and went out, and they found themselves sitting in the glow cast by the kerosene lantern in the middle of the big old kitchen table.

The storm shrieked outside, and the past and the present felt mixed and confused. Rasputin jumped onto Mia's lap and watched the old lady cavort near the ceiling. "They're coming home, see they're coming home!" she crowed.

Chapter Seventeen

"HURRICANE ARGO IS EXPECTED to make landfall on Rhode Island within the next several hours. Wind speeds have decreased to 95 miles per hour. All models are projecting a category one storm with an accompanying high tide surge. Power is out from New Jersey to southern Maine. Do not attempt to travel."

Ann flipped off her cell phone after getting the most recent forecast.

"Maybe we should be saving our batteries. Think we'll lose the internet as well as the power?"

The wind sounded like a freight train running through the house. The lamp shone on the table and Johnny held up two old, leather-bound books he had retrieved from the library.

"Your name Maisy comes from Mehitable." He handed Mia the ancient bible. "This records them. It's a veritable Mehitable-fest in there, and Maisy Hale was the last Mehitable before you." He held up the second book.

"This is her story."

They were safe in the kitchen, but buoys far out at sea were recording record waves while the wind screamed and the ocean knew a rare fury. The wind drove the tide inland, moving everything before it, and beaches, creeks, and marshes were reconfigured in an instant. Further inland, the trees began to break or fall to the ground so quickly and heavily their roots popped up behind them. Silver Beech felt like it sat in the vortex of a tornado, and for the people there, the world narrowed down to the oasis created by the lamp on the kitchen table.

"This is Maisy's journal. It's a record of her life, the story of her two boys—one of whom was your Thomas—and the October Gale of 1870," Johnny said.

"The one thing I haven't found in the house is a picture of Maisy Hale, but if I have it right, you're her granddaughter by a few greats, Mia, and in saving the Nickerson land you are preserving her greatest legacy. She called the land her mother's portion, and the promise to preserve it started in memory of her mother, who considered it sacred and didn't want it cleared. That's what the brothers fought over: to clear or not to clear. Sound familiar? There isn't much new under the sun, is there?" He handed the journal to Mia and emptied the last of the wine into their glasses.

Mia opened the book carefully as the fury of the wind increased. The house seemed to be swaying and the wind was finding its way inside as the house was pelted by debris outside.

"Maisy's father agreed to 'leave her favorite part untouched, the land directly adjacent to our house and the surrounding gardens, from the path in front to the marsh and the ocean behind,'" Mia read.

"Trees are falling out there right now, listen—" Old Pete said, putting a hand to his ear.

"Maisy wrote that this house's central chimney holds it down in a storm. I'm going with that," said Johnny.

The Nickerson land made a natural hollow between its highest point near the house and its lowest point at the marsh. The wind had become trapped there and was rotating as a cyclone and tearing up any weak tree in its path. It was a once-in-a-generation cleanup that would leave only the strongest trees behind. The air was full of leaves and branches and even boughs, and the deer family hid low behind the rock deep in a thicket of underbrush.

"Here's the land-use dispute: 'What use is an old promise? They're both long dead, and none the wiser! It's pure profit. Look around you. We don't need the woods, we need fields and sheep!'" Mia read from the journal.

"Oh that's it, I can hear my brother there. It's pretty much what he said when he told me he'd sold the land. Oh, I'm so sorry, Olive!" Mia said.

"Johnny's right, there really isn't much new under the sun, is there," Olive said and shook her head.

"That's why it takes a lot to surprise us historians," Johnny said archly.

By now everyone was focused on the story in the journal and trying not to listen to the raging wind.

"Storm like this took down the *Whydah*," Pete said.

The seas around Cape Cod were littered with shipwrecks, and the pirate ship *Whydah* was its most famous. Its captain, Sam Bellamy, had sailed through a gale to find his lover, Mary Hallet on the outer Cape, and she had watched from the dunes as his ship was pulverized by the wind and waves just offshore.

"Question is: did Mary Hallet call down the storm in revenge for Bellamy leaving her there? Was she holding the lantern to guide his ship onto the bar to wreck it, or to warn him off?" Pete felt a chill in his bones. He had a feeling these were the sorts of questions you could figure out once you died and everything became clear somehow.

"Think these storms can be conjured?" Ann said.

"Imagine! Before proper forecasting, it probably seemed they could. Maisy writes about how the Puritans thought the devil was in the woods, after all. And right now, at this moment, I have to say, I'm wondering," Johnny said.

"In a way, we have called it down, all of us," Mia mused. "This storm is stronger than it would otherwise be, due to climate change, and it's probably going to do more damage for the same reason, and ultimately who is responsible for that?"

"Here it is, 'the October Gale in 1870. The day dawned dim and gray, without sunshine, but we didn't think much about it at first,'" Mia read.

"So no one knew what was coming, they didn't have a forecast, and no one knew to come in off the water, pull boats, and hunker down. That made it all the more dangerous," Johnny said.

"Even I remember when we didn't have accurate forecasts," Pete said.

They could hear the silver beech out front protesting in the wind, and they could hear other trees snapping around them.

"Oh god, just after she sees the boys for the last time she writes, 'An hour later the sky darkened though evening was still far off. The wind screamed in from the northeast, driving heavy rain and hail before it. The trees screamed outside and the air filled with the debris of anything not tied down and broken pieces of trees. It was a terrifying gale, and it was coming in on a full high tide, and all I could do was stay well away from the windows after the first one broke in the dining room,'" Mia read.

They listened to the raging storm, and Rasputin watched the old lady as she watched his people huddled around the table in the circle of dim light.

JEAN's DREAMS were made of the sound of the wind and the rain, and she saw herself swim like a fish under the waves in the heaving ocean. Lars was still there, and she understood finally that he was caught. Then she saw herself cut the ties that bound them together and bound him underwater with a huge pair of shears. As he broke free of the ocean, she watched his dwindling form swim straight and true for the surface, and despite the raging storm, she knew true peace for the first time in years.

MIA CONTINUED to read from Maisy's journal: "'I waited with the cat, otherwise the house was empty. We heard the silver beech to the right of the front door crack and it was a loud death crack, and the wind carried the top of the tree away from the house to the field across the street. I had always thought of that tree as young Matthew's tree, and it was Matthew's body we found after the storm under another tree on mother's portion, and we never found a trace of Thomas at all.'"

THE WIND WAS STRONGER NOW, and as Mia's voice died, there was a new sound—the urgent screech of a breaking tree —and they knew the second silver beech had fallen to a storm. They waited for it to hit the house, but the impact never came as the tree was blown clear by the wind.

Olive ran to the window and peered out, but it was too dark to see. What would Silver Beech be without its tree? Had the house lost its protector? She didn't want to think about losing the comforting spread of its branches that seemed to hold them close. Other trees were breaking too, from the sound of it, and she backed away from the window.

LARS OPENED HIS EYES. He could see. He moved his hands and they worked. He took a deep breath, and suddenly a million loud beeps erupted and lights flashed, and his mother grabbed him and started crying.

"I knew it! I knew it, you're back. Oh, Lars!" she said.

There weren't enough happy tears. The room filled with doctors and nurses, checking his vital signs, making sure. He felt like he'd been asleep for years. As he began the slow work of piecing things back together, he heard the raging storm and remembered his dreams of riding the waves, and thanked them for bringing him back.

"MAISY SAYS whole villages lost their fishing fleets in that gale. The wind and the sea took them. Here: 'Many lives were lost that day in North Bay and on Cape Cod, and my boys are still among the lost,'" Mia read.

"I found their graves in the village church. I'll take you up there," said Johnny.

The wind changed. Suddenly it was quiet.

"The eye is passing," Pete said.

A hurricane is a revolving circle of energy, and there is always a calm point, called the eye, at its center. The silence was deafening after the screaming winds, and nothing outside dared to move.

"Not sure how long it will last," Pete said.

Olive turned on her phone for the forecast and learned that the storm was passing over Cape Cod and heading into the Gulf of Maine. The current radar map showed the eye directly above them. Before she turned her phone off, it rang.

"Oh, Olive, he's back. Lars is awake!" Elea was crying into the phone.

Olive whooped and jumped into the air and shouted the news.

As the storm's eye passed and its fury renewed, there was little sleep to be had through that long night, but it was still a celebration for Olive with Lars back and the Nickerson land secure.

In the end, the wind receded, and one by one, they fell asleep as it quieted. At sunrise, Olive beheld an altered world. Whole trees and monstrous branches littered the ground, the electric lines were down, and the air was cool and clean. The crippling heat and humidity had been pushed out by the storm.

Pete was up early, too, and when they took their coffee out to sit on the porch steps, they found that only part of the silver beech had been sheared away by the wind. The trunk was still solid, and most of its branches were intact. The house is still protected, Olive thought to herself.

"Let's go see Lars as soon as the roads are clear," she said. Luckily, their cars sat unscathed in the field by the barn.

It's going to take some time to clean up this mess, Pete thought. He could see his garden across the street and there was a big chunk of the silver beech sticking out of it. At least it hadn't hit the house. Pete regarded the mess. Suddenly they both looked toward the Nickerson land, and Olive ran ahead to where the bulldozers waited. At first they couldn't see them. Looking closer, there was just a hint of bight yellow paint under a heavy pile of branches, brush, and marsh grass. The wind had buried the bulldozers deep in storm debris and stripped the pink ribbons from the trees. There was no sign of the posts and it would take weeks to uncover the bulldozers.

Pete smiled at Olive.

"The wind and the sea take, but on the other end of it, they give," he said.

Chapter Eighteen

THE FAWN WAITED in the new quiet for a long time before sticking his nose through the brush that had covered him and his family as they crouched behind the huge rock in the deepest thicket. He smelled salt and brine and wet earth, and he sensed the air pressure was too high to bottom out again and bring more violent weather anytime soon. He sniffed again and didn't detect any human beings, and because he was young and impulsive, he was the first of the deer family to emerge after the great wind of the night before.

His head moved around as he surveyed the altered landscape. The stone walls were still there, and the rocks, but the water had driven sand up where the day before there had been marsh grass. It had spilled far beyond its usual bounds, leaving a line of seaweed and dead sea creatures. Above the marsh, there was a tangle of downed and uprooted trees, and some areas of brush had been flattened by wind bursts. He picked his way delicately through the debris and listened as the first birds began to call tentatively, and as the smaller creatures in the woods began to stir, he lay himself in the sun to rest and soak in its warmth.

ANN WAS IMMENSELY grateful for the propane ring Johnny had hauled out of the barn with the kerosene lamps before the storm, and for the can of Maxwell House coffee Olive and Pete had already broken into. Because of her north shore childhood, she was no stranger to drastic storms. She had grown up on legends of the Perfect Storm, called the Halloween storm on Cape Cod, which had caused unmitigated destruction across New England and sent the Andrea Gail, a fishing boat out of Gloucester, to the bottom of the sea. The storm had driven out her final cobwebs, and her chowder recipe was ready to commit to paper. It was the culmination of every chowder she had tasted and every chowder she had cooked, combined with the wisdom she had gained from Macy at the Sea Urchin. At the old kitchen table in a house still standing but surrounded by debris, she was grateful for the small things. She sipped her coffee, took up her pencil, and began to write in her notebook: Entry, *Boston's Best* 2021, Recipe for New England Clam Chowder from the Quahog Connection, by Ann Marston.

THE POWER WAS OUT ALL over Cape Cod. Streets close to the water were covered in sand, and along the waterfront, several houses were simply gone, eaten by the ocean. Live power lines danced from downed poles, and everywhere you looked, trees lay across cars, roofs, and roads. Amazingly, no one had been killed. And through it all, the hospital where Lars still lay managed to retain a sense of normalcy as he sat up and demolished a plate of scrambled eggs. Head trauma remains mysterious, and while they were watching him closely, Lars' doctors were hard-pressed to find anything wrong with him.

"Soon as the roads are clear and the power is sorted out, we can go home," Elea squeezed his hand, "and not a moment too soon. You've been here almost two weeks already!" She hid the fear and anxiety of the past days with a bright smile.

Almost two weeks. To him, it had been no time at all.

"Olive Adams turned up here as soon as she heard about the accident. She's been here every day to check on you, at least till the storm stopped her," she added.

As he rested after breakfast and felt his strength gathering, Lars remembered a pair of green eyes and a brush of red hair. Then he remembered leaving the Sea Urchin too fast on his bike, with unsaid words on his tongue... He reached for his cell phone and dialed Olive's number.

"Am I too late?" he asked when she picked up.

"Too late?!" Olive couldn't disguise the happiness in her voice. "We've all been waiting for you to come back!"

"Am I too late—for us?" Olive heard a mixture of uncertainty and regret.

It rushed back to her.

"Oh, Lars! I shouldn't have stormed off like that. I've wished a thousand times I'd just stayed and listened. I understand now, I'm so sorry about what happened."

She sat on the porch steps overlooking the storm debris and felt the warm sun and the still air.

"Olive, you have no reason to apologize! I was an idiot, tearing off on my bike like that! I'm sorry, too." Hearing

Olive's voice, even over the phone like that, was strong medicine for Lars. Hope began to replace the uncertainty.

As they spoke, Olive felt the anxiety of the past weeks drain away, and the countless daydreams she had suppressed since meeting Lars began to resurface. She looked over toward the Nickerson land.

"When are they releasing you?"

"Soon as the roads are safe."

"Are you up to coming here and meeting someone? It's about the land. You won't believe what's happened. All good."

His only remaining symptom was the slightest of headaches.

"Of course!" He couldn't wait to see her.

"I have so much to tell you! We have a lot to catch up on, Lars. There's so much we might have missed," and she meant it in every possible way.

OLD PETE PICKED his way carefully back across the street with Rasputin at his heels to assess the storm damage. He'd seen plenty of bad storms, and while he wasn't easily dismayed, he was grateful when the radio reported no known casualties. That was the difference today's accurate forecasting made. He saw that his house had held with little to no damage, but that was no surprise. Old Cape houses like his were built close to the land to keep them from blowing away in a gale. He had lost a few trees outback, but the real problem was the huge branch of the silver beech impaled in his garden. It had landed on top of the pumpkin vine and now obscured it completely. He'd been worried about just this sort of thing happening, and no forecast or preparation could have prevented it.

"Whataya think of that, Raspy?" For a moment he wondered if Eartha had been involved. It sure had seemed like ghosts were walking the previous night, and her sense of humor had run to the perverse. Sometimes she sat on his shoulder, he was sure of it. He smiled at the memory of their time together when they were young, and later as they aged across the street from each other and each grew their own gardens in a spirit of affectionate competition. Rasputin regarded him solemnly with infinite cat wisdom.

DOUGLAS DUNN HATED WAITING MORE than ever. He had gone up to Don's cottage as the storm intensified and now sat on a rock staring at the place were his house had been. Not a trace remained. Everything was gone. All he had was his car and his cell phone, which was pretty much what he had when he began working for Moraine. He spent the morning trying to get the surveyor's crew to come down and begin clearing the Nickerson land, but it was simply impossible. The phone lines were down and the crew had certainly been diverted to storm clean up. Even worse, the Cape was largely inaccessible from Boston. He'd have to tell his boss that not only was the office gone, but plans for the Nickerson land were also stopped short.

Mia and Johnny slowly and carefully made their way through the village to collect her things at the B&B. There was no question that she should stay on at Silver Beech through the storm cleanup and the next meeting of the Historical Society. As they walked and Johnny kept a running tally of the damage, Mia was struck by the timelessness of it all, and how she felt herself fitting into it. Suddenly she had a room at Silver Beech in a house that felt like home in a village she was sure she recognized on some visceral level. The element of water called to her in a way fire never had, and sun-scorched California seemed like a foreign landscape to her now. She wished again she had come here much, much sooner.

They had to climb over a few fallen trees and make their way very carefully around the downed wires.

"This might be the worst storm I've ever seen," Johnny mused, "but I'm from Boston. In the city, storms never have this kind of punch. There's something so exposed here."

"What would California give for the water this one storm dropped alone!" Mia noticed how the parched lawns were already reviving.

Johnny was still a bit surprised to find himself walking through North Bay with the latest Mehitable in the wake of a once-in-a-generation storm. The links and the congruences were unlikely, really quite astounding, but there they were.

"I wonder if there isn't a place for Save the Land on Cape Cod?"

"Oh! Marvelous idea! Of course, there is! Mia, you'd be amazed at the number of people working to preserve what's here! Each Cape village has its historical society. I'm working with the North Bay Historical Society on a project involving Silver Beech—I guess involving you, too, indirectly. There are other land trusts here, too, and they do valuable work. So does the local Historic Preservation board. But the pressure from developers is always there, and sometimes it's just too much."

MIA TRIED to see herself here long-term. She imagined the Save the Land office in this very village, and herself in it, living near the water.

"Johnny, have you thought of living here full time?"

"That's the Cape for you! Pulls you right in! Not sure I could completely leave Boston, but I could spend a lot of time here."

As they made their way down Main Street, they saw a delivery truck in front of Maki's store. The back was open and someone was passing out bags of ice.

"How did that truck even get here? Who can drive? I'm not sure the bridges are even open," Johnny said.

People were out surveying the damage and beginning to clear up. The marsh beyond Main Street had overflowed into village basements—the cleanup was going to be horrendous and take time. There was nothing like major storm damage to bring people together; the effort was communal, and the bags of ice were shared freely, to prolong precious refrigeration until the power came back on.

Mia's host at the B&B was relieved to see her in one piece when she dropped off her keys. "Almost called out a search party!"

"Wasn't there a huge house there?" Johnny pointed at the bare sand on the waterline next to the harbour.

Maisy wasn't sure, but a passing man stopped and shook Johny's hand. "Glad you're good," his new friend Sean said. 'That was Douglas Dunn's McMansion right on the water. Stood out like a sore thumb and was big enough to use for navigational purposes. There's not a trace of it left. The sea devoured it."

"Douglas Dunn the developer?" Johnny asked.

"Yep, The Axe," said Sean, "Apparently he was out at the time. No one's seen him, though. Hey Johnny, a bunch of us are heading over to the Urchin once it opens, want to come along?"

"Yes, Sean, sounds good," he smiled.

Sean nodded to him and then to Mia before dashing away.

"Ice!" Johnny said, and continued back to the heavily laden truck to score a bag and they hauled it back to Silver Beech along with Mia's things. Mia spent the entire walk home scheming on how she could stay.

TREE CREWS and electric crews from several neighboring states descended on the Cape and worked feverishly to return North Bay to the grid. The noise of the chain saws and trucks and other heavy equipment sent the fawn deep into the Nickerson land. Everyone at Silver Beech put in a full day in the yard and outside of the house to return things to normal. And finally, the next morning, Pete and Johnny addressed the old beech tree in front of the house. Pete had the saws and Johnny had the eye for where to trim to make it beautiful again.

"Imagine if there were still two of these beeches out here? You'd never be able to see the house for the trees!" Johnny said. It didn't take much, a bit of reshaping and refining, and you'd almost never believe that a large chunk of it was still embedded in the garden across the street, totally obscuring an enormous pumpkin vine. They'd get to that, too. In the meantime, Johnny hauled the porch furniture back out and repaired the ripped screens. Just as they all were taking a welcome break, Lars Salo pulled up in front of the house, this time in a car, and Olive ran down the porch steps to greet him under the silver beech.

Chapter Nineteen

THE FAWN PEERED out from deep in the brush as the full moon rose over the marsh and the constellations wheeled across the summer sky. He could sense people approaching, and as he retreated deeper into the trees, he saw a flashlight bobbing and heard the occasional low murmurs of conversation carried on the warm breeze.

"A few nights ago it was chaos out here. We could hear the trees breaking from the kitchen."

"A few weeks ago it was slated for clearing."

"A few days ago we weren't sure you were coming back."

Olive and Lars held hands and walked slowly along the Nickerson land after a festive dinner on the porch at Silver Beech. The night was still and peaceful as nature rested from its recent fury. The only sound was that of the crickets and frogs and other nocturnal creatures going about their business. They held hands a little tighter.

"This land is alive, I can feel it," Olive said.

Lars felt it too, though it was hard for either of them to

articulate the sacredness of what they trod upon. There was magic here, and an ancient, knowing energy.

"We're probably walking on a ley line or some such," Lars said, only half in jest. The wind murmured through the trees and the moon shone out over the water to illuminate the landscape. They came to a place by the stone wall where the tall grass had been smoothed down and settled there to admire the view.

"I kept seeing you when I was unconscious. Your eyes, and your hair," Lars touched her hair, her face. Her green eyes reflected the moonlight and were the color of all the leaves on all the trees.

They leaned back upon the grass into their first kiss. The moment was enchanted—until a small deer exploded from the brush, sailed over their heads, and vanished into the marsh below.

Olive shrieked as her eyes filled with the underside of flying deer and dangling hooves, and then she laughed. "I think we've taken his spot!" There was grass in her hair, and Lars was speckled with the leaves and twigs left in the fawn's wake. They felt the pulse of the land beneath them and the pulse of the life around them and within them, and they settled down again upon the grass.

As they reached for each other, they didn't think about the fullness of the moon above and they didn't hear how quiet the night became, and they didn't notice the ancient stag, grandfather of the wayward fawn and guardian of the sacred grove, watching silently by the stone wall to receive the blessing of their joining as it consecrated the land.

THE NEXT MORNING, Old Pete's pumpkin plant appeared to have tripled in size. It seemed to be using the fallen branch from the silver beech, which they hadn't yet managed to clear, as a natural trellis. It was hard to see the branch at all for the great pumpkin leaves and tendrils of the prodigious vine and the tiny pumpkins it supported. Maybe this would be his year, after all, he mused, imagining the big blue ribbon on the pumpkin and how it would look in the picture in the newspaper. His musings were cut short by Rasputin, who was patrolling the garden's periphery for rodents, and he began to see about saving what summer vegetables he could. Everything seemed to be bouncing back, and he didn't see the tell-tale signs of saltwater damage as he had feared. Everything around him seemed energized and green and healthy. He wondered if perhaps the hurricane had somehow revitalized it.

As SOON AS the electricity was restored, a full five days after the storm, Mia took a gloriously hot shower and then arranged to meet with Moraine Land Development, LLC. She had considered calling the number on Douglas Dunn's business card, but she knew from long experience that it was much more expedient to bypass the developer's representative and go straight to the horse's mouth. She had traced Moraine to a small office in New Haven, Connecticut, and a man named Amon Davis. From what she could see, its lifeblood consisted of buying up virgin property to resell as developed land. She had to be satisfied with a zoom call, as much of the East Coast was still reeling from the impact of hurricane Argo and travel was difficult.

IN THE EVENT, Amon Davis was a small man behind a desk, peering myopically into his laptop screen. Mia marvelled that such seemingly insignificant men could wreak so much havoc on the environment.

"Mr. Davis, I want to buy the land on Cape Cod known as the Nickerson land according to the terms proffered by your representative Douglas Dunn at the North Bay Historic Preservation meeting this July." She knew it would do no good to discuss her opinions on the morality of environmental destruction for profit.

"My offer ensures you are more than compensated for your investment and allows you to avoid any costly legal battles that might evolve if the community resists the proposed development. It's a double win for you."

She watched him carefully weigh the situation.

"How much?"

She gave him the figure.

"Done," he said. It had only ever been about profit, and here was one bird in the hand holding a large check instead of two birds in the bush hoping for the best. She marveled again, this time at how much good a large check could do if wielded properly, and they began arrangements for the purchase of the property by the Save the Land Foundation.

"I WANT to appoint you the legal guardian of the Nickerson land," Mia said.

She and Olive were walking along the tame side of the stone wall behind the house. Olive grinned privately at a patch of trampled grass on the far side, and then made for one of the Adirondack chairs facing the marsh. Guardian. Somehow that sounded right.

"We can put it back into a trust, as it was before, only this time with Save the Land, so it's safe. And if you and Lars are willing, it will be doubly safe with your added protection. Your only job is simply to keep it as it is. Like the old promise in Maisy Hale's journal."

They sat together and watched the water. The tide was beginning to fill the marsh and the air smelled of salt. Seagulls milled above looking for clams, and the breeze was gentle.

Olive thought about old promises and new promises, and then just the general promise of everything.

"I'll sign up for that," she said. When she had first come to live at Silver Beech she hadn't been sure she could stay. Now she felt as if she had never lived anywhere else. She had joined her future to it, and keeping the land and the house was now as natural to her as breathing.

Lars loped down the lawn and joined them. He took Olive's hand.

"Guardian of the land? Perfect. I'll help however I can." They looked at each other, and then out over the tangle of forest and marsh and field beyond the stone wall.

"Mia, Save the Land has done a wonderful thing here. *You* have done a wonderful thing here. Thank you."

Mia smiled at Lars. What she had done was simply the right thing.

"That's what Save the Land is for. Actually, I want to move Save the Land here, to Cape Cod." She felt a deep connection to this place and these people, and California seemed very far away.

"I can't think of a better place for it!" said Lars.

"You want to stay?" Olive asked. It was a feeling she shared.

Mia nodded, and Lars said, "Actually, there is some office space just about to open up in the village. Should we look into it?"

"Absolutely!" said Mia.

"And you can stay on at Silver Beech as long as you need to," said Olive.

WHEN JOHNNY WAS ALMOST FINISHED CATALOGING the library, he decided to take a break and check out the attic, thinking he could check for any leaks in the roof at the same time. The attic stretched the width of the house and the window at the back looked out above the trees onto the water. The huge central chimney ran up through it and Johnny immediately began to imagine the space as an airy bedroom, or a book-lined hideaway, with a wardrobe in it leading to Narnia. If it was painted white and the floorboards were oiled—

His reverie ended when he stubbed his toe on something very solid. It was a small chest, very old, made of solid wood, and painted glossy black. It had tarnished brass handles and looked like one of those old ammunition chests a client of his collected up on Beacon Hill. He tried to lift the lid, but it held fast. He couldn't tell if it was locked or if it was simply frozen from time and disuse, so he put it aside and continued looking around. He found a pile of *National Geographics* from around the time of the First World War. He sifted through them and they showed other worlds. Lawrence of Arabia astride a camel with Winston Churchill and Gertrude Bell at the pyramids, Niagara Falls in black and white, the African savanna, and the great whales of the sea. He found old furniture, and a few oriental rugs with potential, and then a collection of photographs he wondered if Olive could identify. He'd have to catalog it all for the Historical Society, and he began to imagine a possible exhibit. He checked the roof, finding it solid and dry, and finally, he scooped up the chest and went downstairs, determined to open it with whatever tools he could dig out of the barn. What else does anyone do with an old, mysterious, and very closed chest from the attic of an old house?

RASPUTIN WATCHED Johnny haul the chest outside, and the old lady watched too, and then she began the most curious of dances way up in the air along the point where the ceiling meets the wall above the kitchen shelf.

"It's been so, so long a time, and I never told anyone," she said to Rasputin in her special way.

"Thomas and the land! The land and Thomas! I'm going traveling soon, I just know it!" and she cartwheeled herself across the ceiling and into the dining room.

April 1871
San Francisco

Dearest Mother,
I am here and well, and certain to never return.
When the tree fell on Matthew that terrible night, I
was standing six feet away from him. It happened
instantly and there was nothing further to be done
about it. But I am certain it won't look that way to the
law and am loath to give up my freedom, nay possibly
my life, and in the end, have both your sons go early to
their graves.

Mother, I am sorry. Keep this letter quiet.
Your loving son,
Thomas

"Marvelous! Maisy always knew! She didn't fully lose Thomas! Oh what a secret to have kept all those long years," Johnny said. They were sitting around the kitchen table while his recent find in the attic revealed its secrets. Ann poured out a pitcher of lemonade and passed some fresh peaches around, but all eyes remained riveted on the chest.

Johnny pulled out another letter. The script was fancy but bold, and the ink faded black.

December 1873

Christmas Greetings to you Mother,
I am well and have partnered in business with
another from New England. We watch the lust for
gold burn bright and sell prospectors the equipment
they need to satisfy it: picks, shovels, rakes, sieves,
canvas, burlap, and beans. There is dust and dirt, a
railway in the making, and money to be made...

Mia held Maisy's journal and listened to her distant grandfather's letters home to this very house. She felt a chill and wished for a sweater but was too absorbed to go find one.

July, 1885

Dearest Mother,
This morning were you born of a granddaughter,
Felicity, with a full head of bright blond hair and a
loud healthy cry. She is strong and feeds well...

The letters had been stored lovingly, wrapped in linen and tied with an ancient satin ribbon. They were accompanied by a faded lavender sachet.

Johnny pulled out the last keep-sake, an odd-sized piece of cardboard, and turned it over to find a photograph of a woman seated on the front steps of Silver Beech holding two small boys on her lap. She was wearing a light summer dress and her thick hair was coiled neatly upon her head. One boy was blond, the other was dark, and most strikingly for an era known for its serious photographs, all three were smiling.

"Here they are! Look!" Johnny held the portrait up. "I never thought I'd find this!" He looked again. "Oh, look! See the two seedling trees flanking the porch steps?"

"This is my family story. No wonder I feel so at home here," Mia said.

They sat quietly. It was such an extraordinary story, such a coming together of ties, that even Johnny found himself awed to silence. In the quiet, Rasputin placed himself carefully on the table next to the chest to be closer to the old lady who was spinning wildly above it.

Chapter Twenty

On the first Wednesday in August, the North Bay Preservation Society reconvened to formally vote on the application to develop the Nickerson land. Lars Salo opened comments in his capacity as planning director. He had been back at his desk for three days, and except for the occasional twinge of a headache, he felt fine.

"I move we close the application as it has become obsolete."

Mia took the floor. "I'm Mia Nickerson, of the Save the Land Foundation. Last week the foundation purchased the land from Moraine Land Development, LLC." She handed the society chairman a bundle of papers.

"Subsequent to the purchase, the land has been placed in a trust through the foundation." She handed over another bundle of papers.

"And Olive Adams has been appointed guardian of the property on behalf of the Save the Land trust." She handed over a last slip of paper.

A sigh of relief swept through the room. When it came

down to it, who had wanted to vote to demolish what little land was left?

"Mr. Dunn—" said the society chairman.

Douglas Dunn was furious. He had been holed up in Don's tiny cottage since escaping his own house just before the storm took it. He had lost everything but his car, and Don was only letting him stay because he was paying the bills. He had come to the meeting in borrowed clothes and the last thing he wanted was to show his face. It was hard enough for him to see Lars happy with Olive and to know that Jean's strength was returning every day and she was out of his reach. Of course, he had known in advance that the Nickerson land deal was lost: his former boss at Moraine had informed him and told him in no uncertain terms that he would attend this meeting as his last official task before he was paid a much-reduced fee for his efforts. Moraine didn't have time for big talkers who, in the end, couldn't get around local boards and neighborhood opposition to their plans for development, so his house and his job were both gone with the storm. His smile was cold as he glared at Lars.

"—Mr Dunn, please sign the form to officially close the application."

The process wasn't designed to be humiliating, it was simply protocol, but it was still hard for Douglas Dunn. He scribbled his name on the line, and the society chairman declared the application closed.

"Thank you, Mr. Dunn."

Lars grinned at Olive.

As they left the meeting, the society chairman asked Mia quietly if she was one of *those* Nickersons. The question felt good. She smiled. "Well, yes, yes I am."

EACH DAY that early August was a summer jewel waiting to be admired. The days were balmy and warm, embellished with breezes out of the southwest, culminating in beautiful red sunsets. The evenings were cool and perfect for sleeping. These were the days Cape Codders wait for all year round, and the weather held perfectly as Johnny decorated the porch for a celebratory dinner that Wednesday night after the meeting. He festooned the porch rafters over the table with streamers and bunting left over from the Fourth of July. In the table's center, he placed a massive bouquet of flowers from the garden surrounded by candles with glass hurricane globes. On each plate he placed a single daisy from the Nickerson land. The napkins were antique linen he had rescued from the pantry, and the plates were blue willow. Ann marveled again at how he could transform a simple setting into a beautiful, timeless festivity.

They started with Ann's seafood gazpacho in crystal cups with seafood forks. Johnny picked out a shrimp.

"Marvelous!"

Rasputin came in at Old Pete's heels.

"I've got eight pumpkins on that one old vine bigger'n the cat," Pete said, taking a cup of gazpacho.

Johnny leaped up.

"Two things!" He went to the gramophone on its side table.

"Get Happy, Benny Goodman 1936, recently recovered from the barn," he announced.

The music filled the porch. Rasputin sat next to the turntable and stared fixedly at a point over the table while Johnny slipped into the pantry and returned bearing a tray of champagne glasses.

The cork popped and flew toward the ceiling and

Rasputin watched as it narrowly missed the old lady who was, for once, hanging still in the bunting over the table.

"Almost time," she told Rasputin in his mind. "I feel it now. I'll see you there later. Don't worry."

Johnny filled the glasses and flipped the record over.

"A toast," he announced. No one could match his sense of occasion.

"In April, Olive inherited a house. By late May, the Nickerson land seemed doomed. We almost lost Lars in July. Mia came home, *and* we survived one serious hurricane. And the summer's only half over!" he paused for effect.

"To Maisy. To the Hales and the Nickersons. To an ancient promise kept. To all the creatures and the trees on the Nickerson land. And to us!" They raised their glasses and drank as the music died.

In the quiet, Rasputin watched the old lady leave the house for the first time ever as she flew through the porch screen and up and up into the night, winking like the smallest firefly.

"Goodbye," she called to him, "Goodbye."

Olive shrugged out of her summer cardigan. The porch was warm with candlelight and music, good food and company, and most of all, life.

Afterword

Old Pete

Peter Souza made the local paper that fall with his award-winning pumpkin weighing in at 1,500 pounds. It took three men and a small crane borrowed from the lumber yard to haul it down to the scale in the village, where it was weighed and carved into the year's biggest jack o' lantern.

Ann Marston

Ann Marston became Boston's main chowder guru when her recipe took first prize for the *Boston's Best* chowder award. She used the increased revenue the distinction brought her restaurant to hire an assistant manager.

Johnny Gilmore

JOHNNY GILMORE STAYED on to finish cataloging Silver Beech, and that fall, he presided over a unique interactive museum exhibit at the Historical Society highlighting music. Every kid in town turned up to try out the amazingly old radios, gramophones, and turntables, and suddenly history was cool.

Mia Nickerson

Mia Nickerson took an office in the North Bay where she worked to preserve Cape Cod.

Olive & Lars

The fawn's spots faded as he grew into a yearling and spent more and more time learning at the side of his grandfather the Old Stag, Guardian of the Nickerson land. They often watched from a distance as Olive and Lars walked the acres.

Rasputin

RASPUTIN WOVE his way between Peter's house, Silver Beech, and the Nickerson land. He sometimes missed the old lady, but not for long as similar figures emerged at Silver Beech, which wouldn't be complete without its share of ghosts and black cats.

Ann Marston's Chowder Recipe

Entry, *Boston's Best* 2021, Recipe for New England Clam Chowder from the Quahog Connection, by Ann Marston

For the chowder base:
Bacon (10 slices, raw) thick-cut, good quality. Dice into quarter-inch pieces
Onion and celery (1 cup each). Dice into quarter-inch pieces
Render the bacon in a large, heavy-gauge pan until the fat starts to liquify, then add onion and celery and saute until translucent.
Dried thyme, basil, oregano, white pepper, and tabasco (pinches)
Clam base (¼ cup) (Minor's is a good brand)
Clam juice (3 cups) (look for low sodium)
Clams (3 cups), chopped (fresh or from a fish market, not canned)
Potatoes, (1 cup), diced (Yukon Gold are ideal: not too starchy and they have thin skins, so no need to peel)
Combine all ingredients and bring to a rolling boil, simmer,

and then add roux (unsalted butter and flour cooked in equal parts as a thickener). Stir carefully so you don't break the ingredients. This is the base.

Either cool the base and refrigerate (up to a week) or add immediately:

Half & Half (1 pint). Stir gently.

*Top Secret:

1. Don't add salt because many of the ingredients have their own and adding it would be overkill.

2. Use dried herbs, and remember they are a lot stronger than fresh. The mystery combination is thyme with oregano.

Acknowledgments

Special thanks to Nancy Smith and the Dolphin Restaurant in Barnstable Village for Nancy's clam chowder recipe.

About the Author

Mary Petiet is an author, poet, and publisher. In 2020 she founded Sea Crow Press. A long-time contributor to Edible Cape Cod Magazine, Mary is also the author of *Moon Tide: Cape Cod Poems, Cape Cod: A Writer's Journal, Owl Magic: Your Guide Through Challenging Times,* and *Minerva's Owls*. Her work is frequently inspired by her native Cape Cod, where she can sometimes be found wandering the marsh in all weather.

Sea Crow Press

Amplifying Voices

Sea Crow Press is named for a flock of five talkative crows you can find on the beach anywhere between Scudder Lane and Bone Hill Road in Barnstable Village on Cape Cod. According to Norse legend, one-eyed Odin sent two crows out into the world so they could return and tell him its stories. If you sit and listen to the sea crows in Barnstable as they fly and roost and chatter, it's an easy legend to believe.

Operating from the premise that the small press plays an essential part in contemporary arts by amplifying its voices, Sea Crow Press is committed to building an accessible community of writers and dedicated to telling stories that matter.

www.seacrowpress.com